PASSION IN
THE PINES

PASSION IN THE PINES

JOHN B. THOMPSON &
JACK WOODFORD

CUTTING EDGE

ISBN-13: 978-1-954840-73-7

Published by
Cutting Edge Books
PO Box 8212
Calabasas, CA 91372
www.cuttingedgebooks.com

CHAPTER ONE

THE SKY OVER France was as gray and ugly as corroded lead. It had loosed rain with regularity for the last ten days and now the wind that blew in gusts gave promise of worse to come.

Colin MacAlister Campbell sat on an overturned gasoline can outside the hospital tent and worked his chilled toes inside his G.I. boots. They made a slight sucking sound which he could hear easily over the dull thunder of not too distant artillery. His dungarees were glazed with mud and another darker substance that still gave off a sickish sweet odor which had long since lost its power to upset his stomach.

A noise at his elbow caused him to stir. A doctor who was as dirty as Colin, except for his hands and forearms, grunted at him. "You want to see him now?"

Colin stood up slowly. His gaunt six-foot-three frame seemed like a scarecrow and the sharp lines of his face were sliced into sections by fatigue. The doctor peered, a little startled, as Colin took off his helmet and revealed hair so white blond that it was something of a shock when contrasted with his dark leathery skin and the gray haze of stubble.

"You got him fixed up?"

"No, I got him comfortable. I'm not good enough to fix him up. Takes a higher power to do that. He's easy and I've given him plasma but his guts are in ribbons with two holes through his chest. He'll live an hour or a day." The doctor shrugged sourly and almost fell.

"When," asked Colin, "did you have any rest?"

The doctor cackled hysterically. "Me? Who in hell knows? I don't. Come on in."

"How long can I talk to him?"

"What difference does it make; he's a dead man anyway."

Jack Taradon lay on a cot, covered by a drab blanket, his face tallow white and his eyes staring at nothing. Colin came up and sat beside him on an empty cloverleaf. "Feel like talking fella?"

Jack nodded. "Have to talk and have to cut it short. Not much time. Want to thank you, Campbell."

"Never mind that. I'd have done it for any one. Now what is it you want to tell me?"

"Long story that begins 'way back. I came from Silver River, Mississippi. My dad has something like two hundred square miles of good timber land … good now but wasn't when he bought it." Jack paused and wiped a dribble of blood from his lips. "Got it for a song from a northern outfit that had cut it over. C.C.C. boys fire laned it and reseeded a big part and now it is as good a tract of timber as you can find anywhere." He paused again and lurched as he tried to restrain a cough. He wiped his lips and continued, "I'm no good Campbell. I drank and ran around with whoever I could find and there were always plenty … of a sort. Wrong sort … except Donna."

"Who's she?"

"Come to her later. Better tell you about the Combine that through me got their hooks into Dad … and him with no legs."

"No legs?"

Jack nodded. "Just nubs. Train accident. Well, this Combine—Miller, a tramp ex-sharecropper; Roberts, a sneaky little, small-time merchant, and Belding, a big, snort-voiced ape who's a local product. They own nearly all of Silver River along with a paper mill. They've been wanting to get their hooks into

Dad for years on account of all the pulpwood he owns but he wouldn't let 'em touch it." He paused and gathered strength.

"So they decided to get it just anyway and I was made to order for them. I was always shacking up with some floozie at Mom Platz's Motor Courts and this night was the same as usual except that I still don't remember what happened. The next morning, when I woke up, my blonde floozie, a real live one, had changed to a brunette who was as dead as a salt mackerel and there was Denny Potter standing over the bed making clucking noises with his tongue."

"Who is Potter?"

"Sheriff—an import and put in office by the Combine which not only runs county politics but has a big finger in state politics. Belding was senator once and his finger got too big. Made a scandal but they couldn't prove anything. My own scandal was hushed up and I was allowed to go free ... if Dad would sign a contract with them. He did, of course."

Jack laughed silently. "This is something. Just by dying I make everything all right, on paper at least, because it breaks their hold on him. You'll have to go there, Campbell, and help him though. He's old and they'll do something else horrible to ruin him, take his land and break Donna's heart. You're a forester and you love trees. I'll die easier if I know that a man with your guts and intelligence is on Dad's side."

He coughed and a rush of blood choked his mouth. Colin took a towel and raked the clotted stuff away from his lips. He breathed a little freer and continued.

"Donna is my niece and I let her fall in love with me. That's the sort of son of a bitch I am, Campbell."

"I guess it's happened before," said Colin softly.

"Not all the way! Hear me? All the way, and if that wasn't bad enough hear me out. The old man cut off my spending money and I made her beg and steal for me and when that wasn't enough I got in debt with the Combine. They own everything, even the bootlegging. Remember that! Roberts, that's his part of the thing—one of them. He runs it in from Kentucky and Tennessee by the tank truck load. They let me get in debt then told me they'd pin a murder charge on me if I didn't pay—one way or another. They even foresaw what's happening now. That's why I say my death *should* fix the old man up but it won't."

Sweat broke out on Jack's face. "This is hard, Campbell."

"Take it easy, son … easy."

After a brief rest he continued, "There was a photographer working at the weekly rag so they made it up with him to take a picture of Donna and me. I had told it … drunk you know … that I could do anything with her I wanted. Hadn't, but I didn't say that. So one night when I went home—not too drunk this time—I didn't let Willie help me in the house. I made him go get Donna. She came out and helped me into my room … and it happened. She struggled but not too hard and she had no protection. Just a housecoat on with nothing under it but a thin gown … it tore easily. She's lovely, Campbell, and a big girl. Smooth and tanned like chocolate milk. Her breasts are like fresh ripe fruit …." He shuddered violently. "I'm still a son of a bitch—but I took her there near the big window to my room—our house is a big one-storied affair with short fat columns like business men going to a shower in the Y—I took her and that dog of a photographer took a shot of us. That wiped out my debt. Watch out for that photograph, Campbell. That's all they have now—as if it isn't enough." He sank back out of breath.

He was silent for a long time and when he spoke his voice held a suggestion of that last moist rattle. "Promise …" It was almost a whisper.

"Promise," said Colin, surprised at the sound of his own voice.

Jack smiled. "Tell Dad ... Tell him I didn't scream and beg when I went. Tell him I'm sorry about all of it. Tell Donna ... No don't tell her anything. They hold onto things like that and they shouldn't. Tell her nothing. I want her to forget. Watch your step, Campbell—they would as soon frame you—kill you, as not. Watch your step .... Watch ...." His diaphragm tightened spasmodically twice, then relaxed like a balloon with a slow leak.

Colin found the doctor. "He's dead!"

"Sure ... told you so. A lot of 'em die."

Colin, cold within and without, went through the flap of the tent out into the dreary gray day. It was getting late and the gray was darkening. His toes squiggled wetly in his G.I. boots as he plodded toward the misty outlines of a hill in the distance.

CHAPTER TWO

Fairview Plantation was one of the many holdings of Charley Taradon's but it was his birthplace so he lived there by choice. It had been built in 1848 and defied traditions of the day by its one-story, sprawled-out architecture but it was cool and comfortable. It was high from the ground and the verandah on a level with the floor of the house was some four feet from the ground. A shelf had been built at the top of the railing from which Charley sat to chew as Donna his granddaughter refused to let him spit between the slats or even in the direction of her rose bushes.

There were four high-ceiled bedrooms with huge fourposter beds, marble-topped washstands and tall armoires. A hall ran the length of the house, dogtrots some people call them, and in the back opposite the dining room was an extensive library. The front lawn was thirty acres of sward and trees of all sorts were overlorded by majestic pines to which had been affixed lightning rods, as pines are notoriously attractive to lightning and Charley loved his pines with a fatherly devotion.

It was dusk and they sat on the verandah after a bountiful supper, listening to the nostalgic cries of whippoorwills, the raspy "speeewwww" of night hawks and a cricket symphony, helped in the distance by the croaks of toads and the occasional bellow of a bullfrog.

Charley sat on his shelf expectorating carefully away from the rose bush, his huge hands gripping the stumps of his legs.

From swinging about in the house on his bars the muscles had developed from those of a normally large powerful man to tremendous proportions giving him a brutally dwarfed appearance. He refused to use artificial aid aside from his bars and on them he was as agile as a monkey.

Donna, clad in faded denim shorts that had once been Levis', sat at the far end of the verandah and said nothing.

Colin let his mind run back two weeks when he had driven up in his jeep, overcome the old man's initial resentment and encroachment on his independence, and had then become fast friends with everyone about the place—Willie, the handyman; Lilla, the cook. All but Donna who, after their first meeting and the explosive event not too long thereafter had maintained a frigid front that kept him at a distance.

She seemed to resent that he had known Jack in his moment of weakness and though Colin had not told her everything the dying man had said, he felt that she sensed that he knew more than he had told. She feared the forces arrayed against them and was outspoken in her belief that they were playing with all the cards stacked and that nothing but grief could come of it.

He had been rather brutal with her about the matter which sent them further apart but that first night as they went into the house they had touched and the electric current that had rammed through them like lightning shocked them into activity that was stupefying. He swept her into his arms and for twenty seconds the tide of emotions rose to flood stage and he could feel the tensed softness of her tall husky body, the ululations of her voice that his lips effectively stopped. Her loins were restless, telegraphing the searing burst of primeval passion that had in an instant rocketed through her. Then just as it had started she came back to consciousness and tore away from him to disappear into the dark hall, a sob floating back to him on the still air. Since then he felt that she actually hated him.

Charley spat, sucked his quid dry, spat again and reaching up swung himself away from the shelf.

"Y'all can sit here as long as you've a mind to but I'm goin' in. G'night."

Colin and Donna told the old man goodnight and a heavy silence descended between them. Colin deliberately got up and took Charley's chair which moved him quite close to her. In the gloom he could see the dim profile of her long healthily rounded legs. There was, he reflected, a lot of them, standing as she did some five feet nine or ten.

"What are you thinking?" he asked with an attempt at gaiety.

"I'm wondering," she said with a chill calm, "what your real reasons are for coming here?"

"The ones I gave aren't good enough?"

"I haven't heard you give any," she replied.'

"If you're suspicious about the speed with which Charley and I managed to agree then you must take into account that we both love trees. After establishing a beachhead like that the rest was easy."

"And out of all the woods in the United States you had to pick on a hidden corner of Mississippi. Pardon me if I seem to think that a little odd," she said.

"I can see what you mean, but you see Jack loved this country, whatever his shortcomings might have been. It was his story—his father with no legs and a burning desire to see his forests saved where they might benefit the many rather than enrich the few. I love forests and I was intrigued by Jack's story. So much so that here I am," Colin explained.

"That's a good reason," said Donna inflexibly, "now what's the real reason?"

"Miss Wadsworth, for some reason which I haven't been able to ascertain, you resent my coming here, therefore no reason I give would satisfy you. We might, however, come to an understanding since I'm here and will be under the same roof with you. I'm going to stay until I accomplish what I came to do. Since I didn't expect you I can do without you and I shall make no demands on you, and if being unpleasant amuses you pray continue. That I have done nothing to deserve your enmity I can prove by the fact that I've been in your presence not more than two hours and during that time I have addressed one sentence to you previous to the present conversation. That in defense for your initial low blow. I can only conclude that you are either a spoiled brat whose fanny needs brushing or that you are a cantankerous neurotic. Frankly, it doesn't matter a lot which, because my business here is not with you. I apologize for my rather blunt speech but I think a little bluntness now might preclude more in the future."

Donna was quiet for a while. "I take it that you have finished your diagnosis?"

Colin rose slowly to his feet. "If you don't mind I'll go to bed now."

The girl bounced to her feet. "I asked you if you had finished," she flared hotly.

"What is the use in continuing this fruitless conversation?" he asked levelly.

"You're trying to ignore me after raking me over the coals and no one does that to me." Her breath was coming in quick, furious gasps.

"Come, come," he chided gently. "Do ladies in this section give way to such plebeian bursts of rage?"

She gasped, bit her lip and slowly sank into her chair. A sob choked its reluctant way from her throat. "Please sit down and talk to me, Mr. Campbell."

Colin suddenly felt repentant, but she had a flair for making him angry. "Certainly." He sat and took out a package of cigarettes. "Will you smoke?"

"Thank you." She accepted the cigarette but from her clumsy handling of it he could tell she was not a smoker. He lit the cigarettes and they sat back, puffing silently for a moment.

"Now, what is it you want to talk about?" he asked.

She squared her chair around and faced him. "Mr. Campbell, if you and Gramp try to go through with this thing there's going to be trouble, bad trouble and lots of it."

"For whom, Miss Wadsworth?" Colin asked.

She bit her lip. "For you, for Gramp, for everyone."

He leaned forward. "Even you?"

She looked him squarely in the eyes. "Yes, Mr. Campbell, even for me."

"We have thought, Mr. Taradon and myself, that as soon as the lease is up we'll have the whiphand," he said.

She stared at him for a moment, her face immobile and expressionless. "Is it possible that two grown men can believe that? If so, then you and Gramp need keepers. You know what happened to Jack. You know that they can trump up almost any charge you can mention in this country and make it stick. You know that you could easily be shot resisting arrest. What on earth are you talking about when you say they can't do anything but accept?"

"We realize all that, Miss Wadsworth. All you say is true. Still the things you mentioned are extremes and will hardly be used except as last resorts. Such tactics are dangerous to use even if they do have the county well under thumb. How, exactly, will our actions make trouble for you?"

Donna came to her feet with a bound. "I will not discuss that, Mr. Campbell. You can go to bed and to hell with you!"

The big high-ceilinged room contained a fourposter bed with a full tester which had been quilted in blue satin many years ago; the cloth had paled to almost white. There was an old-fashioned washstand with a mottled gray and white marble top holding a porcelain washbowl and ornate pitcher; a dresser with a huge square mirror evidently made of solid cherry like the bed and washstand. The furniture had been well kept and showed up a dull rich red in the artificial light.

Colin bathed and leaped into the bed, nude as was his habit. The mattress was buoyant but harder than most modern mattresses. This pleased him a great deal. The nearer things were to sleeping on the ground the better he liked them. He clicked the light out, threw open two more windows and listened to the noisy quietness of the night. Although it was alive with sound from toads, katydids and other insects, such sounds only added to the peacefulness.

He listened for a long time to the whippoorwills, some close, some so far away that their cries were a bare whisper. One was not far from the house in the grove and he could hear the prefacing "chuck" before the main theme, "wills a widow." In the distance came the rumble of a bull spiked sharply by the yap of a cur. The deep melodious cry of a hunting hound sounded in the east like repeated notes of a great organ.

"A summer coon hunt," murmured Colin, smiling as he turned toward the bed. The sheets were cool and smelled of the cedar-lined closet where they had been stored. Colin didn't wear anything to bed and lay on top of the sheets, his brown naked skin savoring the touch of the cool breeze that came from the southeast. He closed his eyes and after a mighty stretch and a quick complete relaxation fell asleep.

After a staggering breakfast the next morning consisting of grits, eggs, hot biscuits, smoked sausage, hot cakes and cane syrup and a cup of coffee which he almost finished, Colin felt energetic and eager for the day's ride. Maude proved to be docile, good natured and willing to help him become a good rider. Her foxtrot was as gentle as a cradle and her running walk was smooth and fast.

"I'm doing all right, Willie ... I think."

"Yassuh, you's doin' all right, but dis hyer brindle critter goin' kill me fo' de day's over."

The roan was as rough as a plowed field and hard mouthed. Colin laughed. "I'm glad it's you instead of me. I don't think I'd last the day. You lead the way and take us to the nearest route to the South. I want to see that section. Miss Donna says we can't do it all in a day."

Willie snorted. "She sho right. Tek a mont' t' see all dem woods ef you wants t' see 'em good."

"Well, I've got to see them good, Willie, and I've got to do it before the tenth of next month. Let's see, this is June fifth, isn't it?"

"Lemme see—dis is a Chewsday and Sunday wuz de ... Yassuh, dis de fif!"

"Well, that gives us a little more than a month. Think we can do it?"

Willie sighed wearily, "Us kin do it all right, but ... Look, how come you don't git Miss Donna to tek you over de woods in de plane? Den you kin see it all and you kin tell mo' bout whut you want to see."

Colin sat upright on Maude and looked around at Willie. "You mean they have a plane?"

"Sho. Jes' 'bout a quwater of a mile back of de hawg barn. Got a little shed back deh fer it and a nice long strip."

"Well, I'll be damned. We won't need Miss Donna. I've got nearly five hundred hours myself."

"You mean *you* don't need Miss Donna? If de Lawd hadda 'tended fer me to fly I'd a had wings."

Colin laughed. "You're riding a horse. If the Lord had intended that you ride four legged you'd have had four instead of two."

Willie scratched his head and was silent for a while. "Yassuh, I reckon dat's right but ... I jes' skeered to death o' dem things."

"We'll see how it goes today," said Colin, taking off his sweat-stained hat and passing his hand over his brow. The day was getting hot as they rode swiftly along a dusty field road and Willie's shirt was already beginning to show spots of sweat. About nine-thirty they entered a dense wood.

"Hit's thick long here cause 'Tater Branch run 'long down deh a ways. We crosses hit in a minute den we gits into de pines," Willie stated.

Potato Branch was a clear little stream, spring fed and gravel bottomed. It was no more than six feet across except where it made deep quiet pools which were almost covered by the green foliage of oak, beech, ironwood, dogwood and wild pecan. The trail wound deviously through the trees and the air was cool and damp.

A mile across Potato Branch they entered low rolling hills covered with feathery long-leaf pines which ranged from a twelve inch tree down to mere seedlings. Tall hickory trees were scattered through them and in the valley, where there was often a small running stream, hardwoods of all sorts predominated. From the crest of a relatively tall hill Willie stopped. "You kin see a long ways frum hyer. De hosses kin res' whiles you lookin'."

Colin dismounted and looked over the miles of landscape. Spotted about at intervals of approximately a thousand acres there'd be a clump of majestic skyscraping pines left as seeders. Occasionally in these virgin trees could be seen the white branchless column of a lightning blasted pine. In the sun it shone as though it had been waxed.

Willie read his thoughts. "Jes' let a pine tree set on top of a hill and de lightnin' goin' git it fer sho. It'll git 'em sooner or later."

Colin pointed toward the opposite hill. "Look at that one. You could have made a fair sized house from that tree. What makes 'em last so long, Willie? Looks like the wind would blow them over after the roots rot."

Willie grunted, "Git on yo' hoss and we'll ride over deh—I'll show you how come dey don't blow down."

When they reached the great snag Willie dismounted and taking a small axe from his saddle he pointed to a root. "Now watch." He cut several large chips out and handed them to Colin. "See how fat dem chips is? Dese ole long leafs don't never rot. Dey's too lightered."

"Too what, Willie?"

"Lightered. Too full of rosgum."

Colin chewed a sliver and the pungent tang of turpentine filled his mouth. It was a clean exhilarating flavor and he chewed some more. Taking the axe from Willie he cut a piece from the trunk. It too was red and sticky with rosin. "Boy, what a fire that'd make!"

They mounted and started riding again. "How far is Lost Creek from here and in what direction?"

Willie pointed South. " 'Bout twelve, fo'teen miles dat way."

"Hell," grumbled Colin, "we're just wasting time riding around here like this. It'll take a month at least."

"Das' what I sed," agreed Willie complacently.

Colin stopped under a gum tree and dismounted, fanning himself with his hat. "Willie, do you know what the old man and I want to do?"

Willie got down and sat with his back against the thick bole. "Not too good, Mr. Campbell. I knows whut they done to Mr. Jack and I knows the boss been layin' fer 'em ever since. I knows de corntrack runs out nex' mont'. I knows dem menses in town and I knows dat dey caint run de mill lessen dey gits another corntrack. I know de boss gon' wring 'em out if he kin."

"Well, that's about the size of it. There's going to be trouble, Willie, and plenty of it and we're going to have to have a lot of help from everyone that we can."

"You sho kin depend on me, Mr. Campbell, and ev'ry nigger on all three plantations. Co'se us caint do much … you know whut de white peoples does to niggers when dey gits outa place, but us'll do whutever us kin. Ole Cap is de bes' white man in de country."

"That's good to hear," said Colin. "I want to know all these things because before long I'll have need of everything I know. Tell me, Willie, what do you know about Miss Donna?"

Willie was silent for a while. "Kinda hates to put my mouf on a white woman, Mr. Campbell. I knows you jus' huntin' fer news but …"

"Go ahead. Something is wrong with her. She hated me from the first moment she saw me and that's all wrong. You can tell me anything you know and it'll stop right here."

"Yassuh, I picked you out for a straight sorta man all right …" Willie was fairly wriggling with embarrassment. "Kinda hard to come out wid it."

Colin said nothing but gave him time.

"You see, Mr. Jack was Miss Donna's uncle." He stopped, sweating.

"Go on," urged Colin.

"Yassuh. Well, when she come to live wid Cap, Mr. Jack was a high rider. He'd come in drunk many a night and Miss Donna would git me to bring him in from de car and put him to bed." Willie stopped and mopped his face with a faded blue bandanna. "Well, suh, one night he wasn't too drunk but I think he jes' liked to have people wait on him. Dat night he wouldn't let me bring him in by myself and wanted me to git Miss Donna to help too, so I done it. She put on a—one of dem long coats what white womens wear and come out to de car. Well, us helped him into his room and she told me to go to de kitchen and git him a glass of cold milk."

Willie looked away and shook his head as though in acute mental pain. "I come back and when I got to a spot in de hall wheh I could see into de room I seen Mr. Jack snatch de coat offen Miss Donna and throwed her on de bed." Willie mopped his dripping face furiously. "Gawd knows I'da give one of my arms ef I coulda missed dat. I guess I jes' stood deh sorta froze like fer a minute or so, den I turnt and run like a rattler was after me. Fo' Gawd, Mr. Campbell, I ain't never told that to another livin' soul."

There was a choking weight on Colin's chest and his sight was blurred. They were silent for a long time each thinking dark thoughts.

CHAPTER THREE

COLIN SAT UNCOMFORTABLY in a rocker and watched the sun sink redly into the treetops. Charley sat on his shelf chewing methodically and spitting into the yard, studiously avoiding the rose bush.

"Smatter with you—tail sore?"

Colin grinned. "That's stating it mildly. I feel like I've been beaten with pine burrs all day."

"What did you see?" Charley asked.

"More trees than anything else. I've seen bigger ones and more of them but I don't ever remember seeing them grow like that ... having been cut over."

"That was the part you rode. When that section was cut the company had started careful methods. Wait'll you see the places where they didn't do nothin' but lay waste."

Donna loped past on her Palomino on the way to the barn and Colin was struck by her superb grace and by the ease with which she handled the big horse.

"Durn handy with a hoss," murmured Charley. "Only one on the place what can handle that damn hard-headed stud. When she was fifteen she decided he was hers and set out to ride him. Handled right off, but one day he seen a mare and just run off with her. Went right ahead and serviced the mare with her on him. She took a quirt to him though and near beat the tail offen 'im. From that day she ain't never had to hit him a lick. He'll eat right out of her hand." He chuckled reminiscently. "Damn comical, though, seein' her settin' on that big bastard and haulin' away while he was stobbin' it to that mare."

Colin wanted to laugh not so much at Donna's predicament but at the way Charley put it. Charley had few euphemisms in his vocabulary.

"Willie tells me you have a plane," Colin said.

Charley slapped his stump. "Sure, and that woulda been the thing, too. You could have flew over the whole area in a couple of hours and you could get a lot better idea of it. Don't know how come I didn't think of it. Got a new Cessna. Had an old Aeronca but it needed covering so bad Donna wouldn't fly it no more so I just got a new one. She'll take you wherever you want to go."

"Thanks, Charley, but we're still biting at each other. I've had several hundred hours so if you don't mind I'll go by myself or take Willie with me."

Charley laughed and spat lustily. "That'll be the day. Willie wouldn't ride in one of them things and I don't blame him. I been flying fer ten years and I still don't like it."

"Somehow I think he'll go." said Colin positively. "You know Willie is a damn good man."

"Sure he is, that's why I keep him around," Charley answered.

"He said that you and I could count on him and all the rest of the colored people to whatever extent they can help."

"That's right. Always tried to treat my hands right and they appreciate it. I have to sit on one every now and then but not often. It always pays off in the long run to treat 'em right. A man's a man; don't make no matter what color his skin is. He got his trials and his troubles and his pride. Take old Albert Macklin over towards Silver River a ways. He ain't settled up with any Negro in forty years. They stay in debt and he won't let 'em move till the debt is paid and they don't never pay the debt no matter how good a crop they make. Then they turn around and steal him blind. Can't hardly blame 'em."

Colin was appalled. "You're kidding. I've read of such things but ..."

"They was so, too. That's why so many colored people are drifting away from the farms and going to town. Every now and then one of my families want to go to town and I always let 'em 'cause it don't take but about one season and here they come askin' me won't I please send Willie after 'em in the truck. I let 'em come back fer the good they'll do the rest, and they're always better fer havin' found out for themselves."

"I'm glad you're not one of that kind, Charley," Colin was deadly serious.

Charley shook his white locks. "Justice is justice. I wouldn't do it to you, to Willie, to a cross-eyed Chinaman, ner to a dawg. I might wring a man out in a trade if he wasn't too smart but I wouldn't put the hooks in him just 'cause I could."

Donna came out attired in a T shirt and a pair of faded khaki shorts. Again the sheer animal beauty of the girl shook Colin roughly. She was big but she was wonderfully curved and finely wrought. Though nature had been more than bountiful it had not been careless or gross.

"What did you do today, honey?" asked Charley.

"Nothing," was her short reply.

The old man shrugged and arched his eyebrows at Colin.

Colin noticed what he had missed under the artificial light of electricity. Her skin was a warm milky tan and her eyes were a startling amethyst shaded by luxuriant copper gold lashes and the brows that arched gracefully over them had never felt a tweezer. They were thick and long, accenting the size of her eyes to a degree.

"Colin is going to fly the plane tomorrow," said Charley experimentally. "He thinks he can tell more about the land that way."

"I think I'll take Willie along with me," said Colin.

Donna laughed a delightfully bubbling tinkle of a laugh. "That I must see. I've never been able to get him up with me."

"That was Charley's reaction," said Colin. The laugh, her first in his presence, made him feel queer inside. "I think I'll get him up though. Willie and I get along."

After supper, when they gathered on the verandah again, Colin said, "Have they made any advances about the lease yet, Charley?"

"Nope. I been waitin' but nary a word yet. I expect it any day now. They're feelin' awful safe or they'd been dickerin' over it before now. I wonder what's makin' 'em feel so good?"

Colin could sense the tension which suddenly gripped Donna even if he couldn't see it.

"We'll find out soon enough, I guess," he said casually. "That's why I want to know every foot of those woods and I want to have estimated every foot of timber standing."

"That'll take a lot of doin'," said Charley skeptically. "Why not git a reg'lar timber estimater to go over it. Old Bob Keller in Silver River'll do it. He knows the land and kin git it done quick."

"That's a good idea. Will you take care of that or shall I?" Colin said.

"I'll call him 'fore I go to bed tonight so's he kin git started tomorrow. I got a rough idea but I'd ruther have Bob's word on it."

"That's right—we want to be on the ball when we dicker with them."

"Well, I'll go call Ben now and go on to bed. Ain't never got out of the habit of goin' to bed early."

Colin lighted a cigarette and inhaled deeply. "I'm sorry, Donna—want to burn a weed?"

"No, thank you."

Colin cudgelled his brain for some way to get her to talk but she was too adept at chopping him down to try any that came to mind.

"Donna?"

"Yes."

"Why were you so much in love with your uncle?"

After possibly half a minute she said, "Mr. Campbell, you have a habit of prying. Were you taught that such a habit is a good one?"

Colin shrugged. "I find that in dealing with you I have to forget what I was taught. We could sit here in silence half the night and nothing would be accomplished."

"Just what do you hope to accomplish?" she asked.

"I'd like to be your friend. I think you need a friend of the sort that you could trust and tell things that sometimes get a little heavy for one person to bear alone. Such a friend is awfully good to have. I have several and I know," he stated.

After another long silence Donna said, "I don't dislike you, Mr. Campbell."

"Colin will do; and if you don't then you put on a good show."

"I resent your coming here and encouraging Gramp to raise all this hell you and he are contemplating. I've gone into my reasons for that."

"And like you accused me you haven't given the real reason."

"And what do you mean by that?" she lashed out savagely.

"Naughty temper," he chided and she subsided in her chair."

"Donna, I'm some older than you are. I've traveled a lot and I've known and associated with many people. Only a fool could do this and not be broadened and tolerant. I think I have a pretty fair understanding of people. I think I could help you. I think just talking would help you. You are unhappy, as anyone can see, and you have it balled up inside of you where it's choking you and ruining your perspective. Your dislike of me was instantaneous and therefore without good reason and I'd like to change that; not for me because I can take life, I've had to, but with you it's different."

"Colin," her voice was soft, "I think you are a very kind person. I think you mean well but you don't know me and I *can't* tell you why I'm unhappy. It's a long and sordid tale. If I told you you'd then hate *me*. People don't like me, maybe because I'm so big and tall; maybe it's because I can beat men at games, things like that. On the other hand, maybe it's because they can see through the front I put up and see the real me. It's not very pretty I can assure you."

Colin lit another cigarette. "Donna, you have just revealed to me how much you really need to talk about yourself. I've seen through you and I can prove it, but I haven't seen anything but an unhappy little girl who needs a sympathetic shoulder and a good cry. I see nothing sordid nor do I see anything else bad."

She sat up straight in her chair. "I was in love with my uncle. Would you call that normal? Would you expect the average girl to have any such feeling for a relative?"

He blew out a cloud of smoke and when he spoke his voice was smooth, rich and soothing. "What is a good standard of normalcy, Donna?"

"Someone," she retorted, "who doesn't have incestuous feelings for an uncle."

"Where is the state insane asylum?" he asked.

"At Jackson, why?"

"It is peopled by several hundred, maybe thousands, of people who are not normal and I doubt that there are any greater percentage of them who have had incestuous urges than in society on the outside. Does that make sense to you?"

"Yes." It was almost a whisper.

"Then your answer falls on its face. Cousins marry every day and their children are not subnormal any more than the children of the rank and file unless there was some anomaly in the blood lines. Such things are not made by incest, rather by genes and chromosomes that the parents carry. Now for the uncle. If cousins can fall in love and marry what natural obstacle is there to a niece falling in love with an uncle? Answer that from a physiological standpoint, not social."

Donna said nothing.

Finally Colin nudged her. "Well?"

"I can't answer it," she said.

"There you are! You don't enjoy being unhappy, do you?"

"No."

"Then let's try to be a little sensible about this. You are old enough to realize that society has erected a code that few if any live by. It's always for the other fellow and the only way it is ever observed is on an average. In the individual there is always war with social codes. Since society will not understand then society must not know. I do understand and as I said I can prove it. Let me pose a theoretical situation and see how closely it fits you. Game?"

"Yes," she replied.

"O.K. Say about the age of … well, nine or ten, plus or minus a few years, it doesn't matter much. You became suddenly aware of a strange leggy gawkiness. Kids teased you about it and poked all sorts of fun at you. You were big and strong and you struck back the only way you knew—physically. You whaled hell out of some of them in defense; you began to work might and main to beat them at whatever they were best at. The boys you tore up on the tennis court, the basketball court, at baseball, running, and anything at all that you could equal them in. You couldn't very well go in for football for various reasons so probably you never liked it and let everyone know it."

An audible gasp came from Donna.

He smiled to himself. "Am I getting warm?"

"Go on," she urged.

"Well, this got to be a kind of obsession. You worked at it so hard that few men could equal you. You never missed a chance to bury them at whatever you could do best. The things you couldn't do too well you affected not to like. The more you worked at this the less popular you became. The girls didn't like you because you made them feel incompetent and prissy. You probably sneered them out of countenance and cut them to pieces with your sarcasm. When you came here you hardly had a friend in the world. Since you've been here you've made few friends and have probably alienated some who might have been so inclined. Now, how right am I?"

Donna rose swiftly from her chair and went into the house.

For a long time Colin sat and listened to the nocturne of nature. It affected him like a soporific and he nodded, nearly asleep before he was aware of it. He stood and gave a tremendous stretch before he went inside. A broad smile activated his mouth as he entered the big hall.

The next morning after breakfast he collared Willie who was attempting to sneak off to the barn unnoticed. "There you are, Willie. Ready to take a spin with me?"

A sickly grin showed the tips of Willie's white teeth. "I wouldn't be no he'p, Mr. Campbell. Betcha I'd be lost 'fo' us was up deh good."

"Tell you what, Willie. You go up and if in fifteen minutes you don't feel all right I'll bring you back. How's that?"

Willie's upper lip became beaded with sweat. "Dat's a good deal awright but …"

"Come on then. Remember, you'll be the first colored man on the place to go up and you'll have it on them all."

Willie perked up a bit at the possibility of enjoying a certain advantage by being the first to coax up nerve to fly, but by the time the sleek little ship was wheeled out and the motor started Willie's nerve had disappeared. "Look, Mr. Campbell, I ain't feelin' so good dis mawnin'. How 'bout me'n you goin' up some other day?"

"Willie," Colin's eyes were cold and uncomfortable and Willie averted his gaze. "You made a deal. Now, let's go."

Willie turned a dirty blue and with a despairing glance at the heavens placed a palsied foot gingerly into the cabin. Colin gave him a boost and slammed the door shut, walked around to the other side and got in.

"Ready to go, Willie?"

"Ch-ch-ch-ch-ch-ch-t-t-t," said Willie's teeth eloquently.

"That's the boy," and Colin whacked the colored man's quivering leg a hearty blow. He glanced at the sock, saw that he'd have a slight cross wind but not enough to give him trouble, and shoved the throttle all the way in. The little ship gathered speed and in a matter of seconds was air-borne. Colin glanced at Willie who was clutching his safety belt with both hands and who had both eyes tightly shut. At six hundred feet he punched him. "You can breathe now, Willie. You're O.K."

It took a while to convince him but eventually he opened his eyes and looked carefully about. A ragged little grin touched his lips. "H-h-h-hit ain't t-t-t-too bad, is it?"

They were flying at a thousand feet over the northern section where Colin could see signs of pulp wood cutting in one area several hundred acres in extent; there were signs of ruthless extermination of everything that grew. Even the scrub oaks which were mixed with the pines seemed to have been ridden down by trucks. Standing trees were skinned, leaned askew and for the most part ruined. They were large trees, some of them would possibly measure twelve to fifteen inches at the butt.

Colin cursed aloud. Prevented from taking out sawing-sized trees they were systematically ruining them. In another six months they would be dead and infested with borers. Colin knew that a mistreated pine didn't live long. He skimmed low over the trees and saw the upturned faces of pulp wood cutters as they stared at the plane. Truck roads had been cut and he could see that they hadn't been used over a few times. Any excuse to cut a large tree and to throw it in such a way as to ruin several more plus innumerable seedlings.

Colin searched the area for a place level and open enough to land but could find nothing suitable so he soared aloft and opened the throttle to its widest and headed back to the plantation. "Hand me that map behind you, Willie. I want to mark that area. I'll bet Charley thinks they're cutting some other place." He took a pencil from the glove compartment and marked the area on the map, checking with the graveled road which ran about three miles from the spot and crossed another a mile further west.

Fifteen minutes later Willie took a mighty grip on himself and endeavored to be nonchalant about the landing. He managed fairly well and by the time they had taxied up to the hangar he was fairly bursting with pride. "Dis hyer de way to travel," he said casually as he climbed from the plane.

Colin grinned. "That wasn't the way you were talking this morning."

Willie shrugged with fine disdain. "A man don't never know till he try."

They started for the big house at a rapid walk.

On the big hall table Colin pointed to the map. "Right in this area they're really mowing it down. They aren't actually logging but they're certainly ruining the place. Skinning trees up by throwing others wrong, clearing roads they don't need."

Charley swung back and forth on his bar and snorted. "They ain't even supposed to be in that area. That's where my biggest timber is."

"What do you think we should do?"

The old man hung by one hand and scrabbled his white hair with the other. "By the letter of the contract we could run 'em off the place and raise all sorts of hell but somehow it looks like that's what they'd like us to do. You see, if they could get us to make some fightin' move before the lease expires that'd be a point they'd make a lot of. Charge us with obstructin' 'em and all sorts of things."

"That's well enough, but about those roads—what became of the logs they cut to make them, there's not a tree to be seen anywhere, tops or nothing. Just clean new stumps."

Charley bit his bottom lip. "If they moved a log my ranger of that district'll know about it."

He swung about and walked hand over hand down the rod into the hall and stopped at the telephone. He ground the hand crank lustily four times and picked up the receiver. He waited some time before getting an answer. "Well, where was you, courtin' some nigger gal? What the hell's all that rampagin' goin' on up there? What they done with them logs they cut for all them roads they been cuttin' that they don't use?"

Charley waited while the receiver squawked and squeaked. "Uh *huh* ... well dog bite my cats. Will Abel let you have the canceled checks? Well, that's just what we want. No, don't do anything yet, but tell Abel I might want them checks and not to leave 'em about where some door smasher kin lay hold of 'em. That's good work, George, and thanks." He hung up and turned to Colin. "Let's go on out on the gall'ry where I kin set."

Colin followed him out on the verandah where a cool breeze was blowing.

"George Hall, he's tower man in that area, says they cut those roads at night and trucked the logs away. He got in his jeep and followed them with his lights out and they took the logs to Walter Abel's sawmill in Centerville. George says there must have been thirty loads in all ... nice little sum they'll have to cough up. Miller and them ain't got a single acre of timber land and yet they had the checks made out to 'em ... rather to their pulp gang boss which'll be the same thing."

"And in the meantime we let them ruin as much timber as they stole?" Colin asked.

Charley massaged his jaw. "Well—reckon you kin stop 'em 'thout runnin' 'em off and givin' 'em somethin' to bleat about?"

"I can go out there," grated Colin, his blue eyes sparkling, "and beat the hell out of whoever is in charge of that deal and take an estimate of how many trees are ruined. You can tell Bob Keller about it and he can go up and verify the estimate, then we'll have him and George and me as witnesses as well as those checks which you'd better send someone to get today. We're going to need them soon and there's no use allowing them to get stolen or lost."

Charley gripped Colin's knee. "I might be doin' wrong to let you go on with this but go to it, son. Wisht they was a mile or so of bars out there so's I could git around and I'd go with you."

"You can go with me. Get your hat and we'll go in the jeep—right now."

The old man's eyes burned restlessly. "By god, I'll do it. Lilla!"

Lilla pounded through the house and on to the porch. "Yassuh?"

"Is dinner about ready?" he barked.

"Yassuh. Will be in 'bout ten minutes."

"Well, hurry it up—*we* got places to go."

After dinner they got into Colin's jeep and departed. Charley had refused Colin's offer of help and used the rod that extended from the house to the yard gate where he dropped to the ground and using his arms like crutches hoisted himself nimbly into the vehicle.

It was three o'clock when they picked up George Hall at No. 4 tower. George was a thin cadaverous individual who chewed tobacco continually and had a pair of sharp amber eyes that never stayed still. He shook hands with Colin limply and climbed in the back of the jeep.

"Jes' take that there road to the right and it'll take you to a mile of 'em then you'll have to go across the woods. Tain't bad drivin'."

"How come you so late tellin' me 'bout what was goin' on, George," said Charley twisting about in the seat.

George shrugged and shot a stream of tobacco juice into the top of a clump of yankee weed, making it sway heavily. "Been thinkin' they was up to sumthin' but I wasn't too sure till that night when they hauled them logs away. They stacked 'em with limbs then one night they come and took the whole shootin' match. I seen the line of trucks from the tower—the lights I mean, then I jeeped over to watch 'em. When they got all loaded I took out after 'em with my lights out and I seen where they was takin' 'em. I parked the jeep a good ways away and snuck up close to Abel's office and climbed a pile of lumber where I could watch good. I seen Abel hand John Prince a check. I waited around till

John left, then I went in and told Abel what the story was and he likened to fainted."

Charley nodded. "He would. Abel is a good friend of mine. I let him cut some of my stuff once when he was on his ass and needed a hand."

"Well, he didn't know what to do but I figgered since it was already cut and delivered all you'd want was the canceled check, so's you could drop a sack over their heads whenever you wanted to, so I told Abel just to keep the check when it come back and to go ahead and cut the logs."

"Good enough," said Charley with satisfaction. Colin could see that the old man had picked his men with care.

"I seen Abel last night," continued George. "And he said he had already got the check back so now all you got to do is get it from him."

"You can run up there tonight and get it," said Charlie, "and mind you stay away from them gals of Jim Stuerm's on the way."

George grinned and didn't reply.

"Who's Jim Stuerm?" asked Colin curiously.

"Oh, Jim's a white man what's got eleven dotters by a nigger woman up in the woods a ways."

Colin scratched his head. "Jesus ... eleven ... daughters by a Negro woman?"

Charley chuckled. "Eleven dotters and two sons. Damndest best lookin' spread of woman flesh as you'll find this side of the Delta. Never seen nothin' like it. But Jim ain't the only one. They's plenty more. The difference is that Jim's kids is nearly white. Lot's of people don't know the difference if they don't know the family. The woman was half white, mebby more, and when the children come they was *all* white to look at 'em. Fine lookin' set of youngsters, too."

"Lot better lookin' than his legal kids," said George expectorating juicily. "*Them's* the dangdest set o' cross-eyed brats I ever seen."

Charley nodded and dodged a stiff scrub-oak branch that slapped at him. "Jim's wife ain't nuthin' to speak of as to looks. She so cross-eyed she kin count a settin' of eggs 'thout movin' the hen."

Colin doubled up with mirth at Charley's analogy and nearly put a wheel in a stumphole.

"Cuss them there scrub oaks," snorted Charley as the branch of one raked him painfully across the face.

"They're good to keep the land from washing," alibied Colin. "That is, if there isn't anything else to do it. Pines would be more profitable but the oaks are better than nothing. They make good cover."

George patted Colin on the back. "Right up here a ways you'll see where I pulled off to the left. Follow my tracks, else you'll hang up on lightered stumps and they'll gut you."

"One thing … 'bout … the war," said Charley with difficulty due to the rough going. "These here things kin go any place a cow kin."

They came out of the gully on the slope of a long hill and there below them was the area Colin had seen that morning. It was fairly smooth going down and in a few minutes they pulled alongside a truck that was being loaded with lengths of pulpwood by four Negroes.

A thick stout-limbed pine had been thrown fifty feet ahead with such pointed carelessness that it had crushed half a dozen seedlings and scarred a long six foot gash in a slim ten-inch tree that in a few more years would make an excellent stock log.

Rage rose in Colin as he looked at this and other evidence of deliberate sabotage of the provisions of the lease.

"Where's John Prince," bellowed Charley who was red faced with anger.

A big yellow Negro grinned insolently. "He round sommers, I reckon."

Colin leaped from the jeep and strode over to the nearly loaded truck. He tapped the man on the chest with two fingers that were as stiff and painful as a tire tool. "Get him and I don't mean tomorrow."

The man backed away and bowed respectfully. "Yassuh ... yas-suh. Sho will rat now."

A little wizened very black Negro came up to Colin. "Dat yaller nigger sho is tuff when ain't nobody 'round bigger'n me." He grinned. "I wouldn'a took a week's pay fer dat. You, Mr. Campbell, ain't you Cap?"

Colin grinned and nodded. "Yes. How did you know?"

"News gits around." The little man looked wistfully at Charley. "Sho wishes I could work fer dat white man."

An inspiration struck Colin. He caught the little Negro by the shoulder. "Come over here for a moment."

The other two men had never stopped loading the truck from the other side but they might come around and disturb Colin's conversation. "This man," he said to Charley, "wants to work for you but he already has a job and I can't see any reason why he can't hold two jobs ... do you?"

He dropped a wink to Charley over the little man's shoulder.

"Er ... why 'co's he can," said Charley, his eyes lighting up. "Tell you what bub. You take this."

Charley handed him a twenty dollar bill keeping a keen eye on the other men at the truck. "Now, any time you hear anything you think I might like to know you find some way to let me know. You don't need to let anybody else know about this. Jes' keep on with your job here and I'll slip you another twenty pretty soon. A deal?"

The little man grinned showing a mouthful of white powerful teeth. "Yassuh. Hit sho is a deal." He pocketed the twenty and scuttled back to the truck.

"Can't beat colored for findin' out things," said Charley biting off a jaw load of Brown's Mule. "Man might come in pretty handy."

"That's what I thought," said Colin. "He doesn't like that yellow one that I had to shake up. Said he was tickled to see him moved around so I figured he'd be a good man to have in the enemy's camp. One with a gripe. And this, I take it, is Mr. Prince."

John Prince was a huge beetle-browed man with black hair and a blue chin. He had the stride of a belligerent man accustomed to driving other men. He stopped a few feet from the jeep and spat insultingly on the grass before him. "What you want?" he croaked in a hoarse voice that had been seared by strong whiskey and strong tobacco.

"I want to know what the hell you mean by beating my trees down and skinning up my standing timber. You'll pay market price for every goddamned one you scratch, and furthermore, where's the logs from those stumps all around here. They didn't walk off."

"We had to make truck roads," barked John, his face reddening. He began to beat his booted legs with a rattan swagger stick he carried.

"Not that damn many truck roads," put in Colin. "I see some of them never had a truck on it except the one that picked up the logs."

"Who're you," asked John belligerently, taking a step toward Colin.

"He's my head forester," bellowed old Charley as red as a lobster, "and answer his questions and mine. Where them logs?"

"I'm in here cutting pulp fer the Silver River Paper Mill, Incorporated. I don't let nobody tell me how to cut wood and I don't know nuthin' 'bout no logs. I cut paper stock."

George Hall slid out of the back of the jeep with the fluidity of a snake. He spat a stream of tobacco juice narrowly missing John Prince's boots. "What about them thirty trucks that was in here four nights ago loading logs and hauled them to Abel Becker's mill in Centerville and that check he wrote and handed you?"

John's eyes opened wide then slitted almost shut. "If you got questions go to the front office. I don't answer none here. I cut pulp wood."

"You said that once or twice or three times," said Colin settling himself solidly on his feet.

"Listen you. I don't know you from a load of pine knots but for my money you're just another meddling son of a bit …" Colin's left shot out like a piston and John Prince swayed in his tracks like a tree ready to fall, then lurched heavily against the jeep where he managed to claw himself erect, his eyes straying about uncertainly in his head.

Charley let go a roar of laughter. "Easy on the rough language, bub. Colin'll jar your ancestors all the way back to Egypt."

George Hall looked on with a quiet grin, chewing rapidly, his hand in his pocket where just for safety he had thumbnailed the blade of a Texas Jack open and palmed it ready.

Prince shook his head and blew like a steam engine, then with the speed of a snake striking he slid a short axe from his belt and aimed a mighty blow at Colin. The blow halted with muscle bursting suddenness in midair. Charley's right had clamped around his arm high on the wrist and was slowly carrying him back. Prince yelped with pain and clawed at the old man's terrific grip on his wrist but the pressure only grew more terrible. Prince now had his back to the jeep bending over backward to keep his arm from being broken. The man's fingers were in a paralytic strut, swollen and purple from the awful pressure being exerted on him.

Charley's face grew dark with blood and he now had Prince almost laid on his back in the jeep. Prince had ceased to claw at the crushing hand because the more he struggled the worse the pain became.

"Now, goddamn you," bellowed Charley almost into the man's face, "you'll talk or I'll wring this here flipper plum' offen you." With the other hand he cuffed Prince a hard cruel blow across the face and on the return he backhanded him with enough force to shatter his teeth.

"Jesus Christ, let me go … I'll tell you anything I know … just let up on my arm."

With a violent thrust Charley shoved the man into a stumbling sliding fall.

Colin picked up the axe and leaned against the vehicle and watched Prince slowly come to his feet. "All right now. Who gave you orders to start this kind of cutting? You haven't been doing it except lately. I've seen a number of areas where the cutting was done carefully and well."

Prince looked at Charley with a strange light in his eyes and tried to rub some circulation back into his bruised wrist. "The boss done it," he said sullenly. "He told me to cut as fast as I could and to hell with the seedlings and stock timber."

"And why this sudden change?" asked Charley.

Prince looked at him sullenly and clamped his lips shut. Again that lightning-like left snaked out and Prince stretched out in the soft grass. There had been no jeep to catch him this time. Over by the loaded truck came a thin snicker from the little black Negro. The big yellow one looked on with fear in his eyes while the other two had stopped loading and were watching with keen interest. Prince sat up slowly.

"You hit me again," he said stupidly.

"That's right. Next time be a little more prompt with your answers. Why the change in cutting methods?"

"Lease up next month and the boss wants to get a stock pile while he's dickerin' with y'all over the lease."

Colin took three steps and stood threateningly over the man. "There's another reason."

"He wanted y'all to put us off the place so's he could say he's been held up without reason. He could get a lotta wood and mebby get run off all in the same operation."

Colin grinned triumphantly at Charley who nodded vigorously.

"What about them stock logs," came George's nasal whine.

"I sold 'em but the boss got the money. I got ten percent."

"That's good enough, Prince," said Charley gloatingly. "You can tell your boss what a mess you made of things but I wouldn't if I were you. He might not like it." He sat very straight in his seat. "All of you bastards 're gonna learn a few things 'fore this year is out. Every damn one of you. Come on, Colin ... George. Gittin' on towards suppertime."

At tower four they let George out and Charley repeated his admonition. "You go on up to Abel's tonight and git them checks and pass right on by them Stuerm gals' house."

"You don't need to worry none," grinned George. "I ain't like you."

"What did he mean by that?" asked Colin as they drove off.

Charley's shrug was too elaborately casual. "Sunovbitch jes' bitin' back at me. He don't know nuthin'."

Colin laughed. "Wouldn't take a bet on that, would you?"

"Shet up," said Charley grinning, "and drive that there car."

CHAPTER FOUR

A THUNDERSTORM WAS building up in the southeast as they drove up the long driveway and pulled up close to the front gate. Colin drove near enough so that Charley could reach his bar, knowing how he despised to be helped.

"Better put this here June bug in the garage. There's plenty of room 'longside of the Dodge. Gonna come a turd floater here in a minute."

"O.K., Charley. Shall I open the gate for you?"

"Hell no. I'll make it O.K. Go on and put up that thing and wash up. Nearly time fer supper."

Colin wondered where Donna was. He hadn't seen her at breakfast nor had he seen her during the day. He knew she was avoiding him and wondered if he had been a little too strong with his analysis the night before. At any rate he had got close to her, something he hadn't been able to do before.

She appeared at supper but was quiet and ate in silence without entering the conversation at all until Charley chortled.

"You shoulda seen Colin clip John Prince in the kisser this afternoon. Knocked him on his can twice. More fun'n a rattlesnake after a one legged preacher."

Donna eyed her grandfather with cool distaste and transferred her glance to Colin who was anticipating it. Their eyes clashed briefly, her's giving way to the steadiness of his.

"You gained something by it?" she asked her grandfather.

Charley chuckled and forked chicken and creamed potatoes into his mouth. "Mebby so, mebby not. Done me a wallopin' lot of good though. Fust time I been in a scrap in years."

"You got into it?" she asked.

"That he did," put in Colin heartily. "He saved me from getting my skull split open with an axe and almost twisted the arm off Prince."

From her face one might have assumed that Donna considered this Samaritan act of Charley's not too good an idea. She went back to her eating and was silent for the rest of the meal. When they went to the verandah after the meal she did not accompany them.

In the southeast thunder rolled and battered at the heavens. A cloud of blue-black color with angry brows frowned heavier and closer. The air was heavy and muggy with hardly a zephyr stirring and all nature was quiet, waiting for the storm to break, with even the crickets and grasshoppers silent. A livid streak of lightning rammed earthward four times and a crackling, rolling barrage of thunder followed almost instantly.

"That'n was close," said Charley, frowning at the dense cloud that was rolling ever nearer. "People say lightning don't never strike the same place twict but that'n struck four times within two seconds. Probably beat some tree to kindling wood."

"Willie says it'll get a pine tree every time," Colin stated.

"That's right. Specially these old field pines what set off on a hill sommers by themselves. That's how come I got lightning rods on these big 'uns here in the lot. Bet they been struck two dozen or so times apiece. Probably get it now in a little bit but it always hits them rods. I got 'em run off a ways from the roots of the tree so's the bolt don't harm them. People thinks I go to a lot of trouble for a tree."

"I don't," said Colin positively. "Those old pines are pretty close to two hundred years old and there aren't many like them any more."

"I figger they're a good bit older than that," said Charley changing sides with his quid. "My great granddaddy settled here in 1840 and 'cordin to my pappy them trees was here then and about the same size."

Suddenly a cool breeze sprang up like the breath from an air-conditioning unit and Charley breathed it deeply. "Smell that rain. Ain't nuthin' like it."

Colin glanced at the old man. He showed unsuspected flashes of sensitivity at times. The breeze grew stronger and the lightning flashes more numerous as the heavy cloud boiled closer. A bolt of livid violet tore a gash in the sky and struck a fence on the hill to the west of the house, dancing along the wires for several hundred yards before leaping off and striking a young live oak. A split second behind it came a cannonading crash of thunder that rattled the windows and went rolling off through the hills muttering and grumbling.

Charley grunted. "That was a waste of effort. That tree'll take many more. Can't hardly kill a live oak."

The wind had now risen to gale force picking up clouds of dust and sending them scurrying along with leaves and brush, reminding Colin of the tumbling tumbleweed of song and fact.

The giant pines thrashed and flung their stiff branches about, shouldering the wind in belligerent revolt. The beeches flowed gracefully with the wind like a clipper ship scudding through the seas with full sail, losing leaves, twigs and fragments of dead branches. Blinds banged at the back of the house and Lilia could be seen flitting from room to room lowering sashes and closing doors.

Charley reached up and caught his rod. "Guess we'd better be gettin' in."

"Go ahead, Charley," said Colin. "I want to watch this a little longer."

Colin stood up and walked to the verandah steps where he faced the howling wind and let it balloon his clothes and cool his skin. Sand whipped up and carried along by the wind like tiny shot stung his face, making him squint his eyes. A raindrop, the size of a twenty-five cent piece, plopped on the brick walk a few feet out, spattering into fragments. Another fell striking his forehead and scattering little droplets of water in his eyes. He wiped it away and was conscious of a kind of animal exultance that seemed to ride out of the storm to take possession of him. He felt that he'd like to mount some wild steed and to race along with the crashing elements and join their prodigal enthusiasm.

In the distance came the muted roar of the deluge but at the house only the scattered giant drops pattered with spaced laziness. The woods to the south and east were blotted out in a gray pall of falling water creeping closer and closer. Lightning skittered and jousted like giants fencing with sabers of flame, and the thunder was the mighty clashing of their blades.

Though the sun had been down only a few minutes the world grew dark and night seemed to have fallen in a twinkle, lighted only by the blazing trails of electricity. Louder grew the roar of the rain and like a man in the thrall of a hypnotic spell Colin walked slowly to meet it. Out of the yard gate and to the middle of the three-acre open space where the driveway had made a great circle, he stood and with a liquid roar the cloudburst came down and wet him through. It came in a blinding choking avalanche that almost defied breathing so closely were the drops spaced. They stung his face like little lancets and beat at his clothes as though determined to tear them from him. Like a carven image he stood and let the water beat through his clothes till it ran in rivulets into his armpits and made broad bands of cold across the hard surface of his stomach and down his long powerful legs. It ran into his shoes to make spudgy sounds when he moved his toes.

Suddenly he was aware that he was not alone. He turned his head to see Donna standing not ten paces away, her face lifted to the pelting water, her eyes closed and on her lips the half smile of utter release and freedom. She was a water sprite returned to its elements, a naiad taking sustenance from the fury of the storm, a spirit lifted and rejoined to the nature which had made it. He was aware that she had not seen him so he didn't speak to her but backed away to her right and out of the angle of her vision.

Seeing her thus affected him strangely as though he were watching her disrobe or bathe ... something he should not be doing. Her clothes were soaked to her skin tight and for the first time he had a clear conception of the utter bodily beauty of her. Her hair wet and sticking closely to her skull showed its fine bony structure conforming with symphonic grace to the classic mould of her strong willful face and the purely wrought column of her neck. Her skin looked eel slick, lubricious from the film of water, its warm brown accentuated. He could see her breasts in his mind's eye even with their translucent covering disguising the fullest detail, taut and hard from the chilling touch of the rain, their nipples pike-sharp striving to pierce their frail confinement.

From chin to ankle she was a poem of grace, the lines of her stomach, hips and legs blending and flowing each into the other with that subtle magic which sculptors have striven to carve into senseless marble. Colin's breath fluttered in a ragged sigh. The sight of her standing there wedding herself to the rain, wind, and lightning sent a shudder of amazed wonder through him. Almost like the superstitious awe of a man standing in the presence of a deity. The breath went out of him gustily and a great resolve took possession of him as he turned silently away and squashed his way back to the house.

An hour later the rain had slowed to a steady patter and the thunder was a senile matter in the distance. Colin dressed in fresh khakis and went back to the porch where he expected to be lulled by the dripping water. The heat of the day had been replaced by a comfortable chill, his skin still stung from the effects of the cold shower and a great peace was in his soul. When he reached the porch he could see the dim form of Donna dressed in something soft, white and clinging.

"Nice rain," he commented cautiously as he took his seat.

"The most glorious rain I think I ever saw," she answered, her voice rich and vibrant.

"Yes, I could tell you were enjoying it."

She wheeled around. "How did you know?"

"I was standing not ten feet from you when the rain was hardest. You didn't see me?"

She shook her head and looked away from him.

"Does that spoil everything?" he asked softly.

She shook her head. "No … only I just … I wish you hadn't."

"You're afraid again," he said, lighting a cigarette. "Are you going to go through life with fear and insecurity spurring you into all sorts of compensatory handsprings and making it impossible even to share the joy of cool water falling on your skin with someone else?"

She faced him, her lips parted and her breath quickening. "Colin—you do understand, don't you?"

"If you knew just how much I do understand you'd jump up and dash off like you did the other night."

"You must think me an awful child … a ninny?"

"On the contrary I know that you have been very badly bruised and that you're trying to come back as hard as you know how. The only thing is you have nothing to help you, nothing to gauge your values, nothing to mark progress. You're trying to whip it by yourself, and, Donna, that just won't do. It's curving inward on you and you reach blank walls too often. *Isn't that right?*" His voice had the crisp crack of a whip.

Her reply was almost a whisper. "Yes."

He leaned over and placed his big hand on hers. "Then, why don't you let me help?"

The sky was much clearer now and the curved sickle of a moon peered out for a moment low in the west. In the new light he could see her face with relative clarity and it appeared sad but moved and hopeful. She placed her other hand on his.

"You are very kind, but please don't rush me. Please let me come along in my own time. I realize that you're the one who can probably help me a great deal but you're still almost a stranger and I ... I'm still awfully mixed up. Let me *grow* closer to you."

He squeezed her hands and withdrew his. "The old know-it-all has been put in his place," he said.

"*Oh, no, Colin.*" Her voice was agonized.

He patted her hand again. "I didn't mean that the way it sounded. What I mean is I should know better than to rush you. I'm pushing you when I should be preparing a path on which you wouldn't fear to tread. I'm sorry, Donna. Just remember that you can talk to me at any time on any subject. I repeat ... *on any subject on earth.*"

"Thank you, Colin ... I believe you."

Through an entire cigarette they sat in silence listening to the world come alive after the rain. Frogs, seemingly by the millions, were telling what they thought about the bounty of nature and the insects, quieted before the onslaught of the storm, were making up for their silence.

"Colin, what did you mean when you said you understood more than I had any idea?"

He thought over his reply, whether he should tell her or not. He decided he would. "Out there in the rain you were a lover and he possessed you completely."

Her gasp was sharp and abrupt. He caught her hand in a hard painful grip. "Steady now. When I said I understood, I did. I wasn't kidding and I'm not one of your rustic blue noses. Don't run away this time. Face it, *conquer* it."

Heat lightning far away to the west showed her face to be wet with tears and she rested her forehead on the back of his hand and wept softly. When she raised her head he stood up, and pulled her gently to her feet. He touched her cheek lightly with his fingertips.

"Go to bed now, my dear, and don't let yourself worry. I know that due to things in the past you feel you're something evil; but believe me it isn't true. When the time comes we'll beat all this—you and I. I understand you, Donna, and I see a fine woman. You have been confused and in the past you might have acted unwisely but that's gone. Go to sleep now and remember that I think you're a most wonderful person."

She uttered a sigh that was half sob and taking his hand in hers she pressed it gently to her soft cheek, then she was gone.

The next day was Sunday and a lazy day in all the South. Breakfast was later than usual; instead of eating at six o'clock it was seven and they probably stowed away more for reason of the extra hour.

They were nearly ready to leave the table when Willie thrust his head through the kitchen door. "Mr. Semple out on de gall'ry. Say he want to see. you when you through eatin'."

Charley grinned at Colin. "Let him wait. He's the lawyer from the paper mill. I guess this is what we've been waiting for. Lilla, pour some more coffee."

"None for me," said Colin hastily. "I think I'd be drunk if I drank another cup."

Thirty minutes later they went out on the porch. Charley dropped into his chair with a thump and said, "Ed Semple—Colin Campbell, my head forester. Now what do you want?"

Semple was paunchy, short and exuded spurious charm. He shook Colin's hand effusively and Colin knew why the lawyer didn't shake with Charley, remembering his own first grip with the old man.

"Oh, I just dropped out, Charley. Sort of social-like on Sunday morning, you know. Ha, Ha, Ha."

"Social, heh? Well, I thought people waited till they was ast 'fore they went callin'."

Mr. Semple slapped his fat thighs and guffawed. "Still the joker, ain't you, Charley? Actually, though, I brought you a check."

"A check for what?"

"Well, the whole thing was a mistake …"

"Musta been," interrupted Charley, "if you're bringin' *me* a check."

"Er … hum … Yes! Well, as I said a mistake has been made and Ben thought it was no more than fair that you be reimbursed."

"Ben thought that, huh?"

"Yes. Awful fair man, Ben. Now, as I was saying …"

"What's the check for, Mr. Semple?" asked Colin bluntly.

Mr. Semple's eyes grew opaque with irritation though his smile was as affable as ever. "Charley, don't you think we could get along better alone?"

"No, I don't," snapped Charley sharply. "I tole you Colin was my head forester. If you want to talk to me you'll have to talk in front of him."

"Oh …" Mr. Semple seemed surprised. "Well, in that case … It's about those logs Price sold, Charley. Seems he thought he could get away with it and felt that if Ben caught him he wouldn't do anything, but that's neither here nor there." He took out a wallet the size of a brief case, extracted a certified check made out to Charles A. Taradon, and handed it to him. "I hope that'll be satisfactory. I think Ben added a little to make up for damages done to your trees."

Charley grinned and handed the check to Colin who looked and pursed his lips in a soundless whistle.

"Must have been Malayan teak they cut instead of pine," Colin said.

"As I said, gentlemen, Ben is most just. It isn't so much for payment that he's giving you such a price but because through his efforts you have been treated shamefully."

Charley took the check from Colin and examined it again. "Nice sum," he said half to himself, then turned to Colin. "Use a typewriter, son?"

"Yes."

"Good. Go make out a statement to the effect that we are acceptin' from Ben Miller and Company a check in payment for logs which Ben claims to have been cut unbeknownst to him and that his check covers the thirty loads of logs … *and* certain damages to surroundin' standin' timber. That the check covers just that and nuthin' else, bindin' neither party to any other consideration either real or implied. You know, make it good and legal. Leave room for three signatures."

"Oh, but Charley, look here … what's the use of all that? After all, Ben is just trying to be decent and …." He made a grab for the check and caught the heel of an extremely hard hand in his Adam's apple that sat him back in his chair with a thump and rendered him speechless for several seconds.

"I don't know what other reason Ben had outside of knowin' I'd git them checks he got from Abel and that he paid Prince ten percent and told him to try to git me to run him offen the place. Ben is fair and Ben is just and Ben is decent. Mebby so, but I'll take a rattlesnake any day."

"But, Charley!" Semple's syrupy voice was gone and he sounded a little shrill. "Ben's trying to do the right thing and ..."

"If he is," trumpeted Charley, "then he won't mind a nice legal receipt fer his money, done up right and signed by all three of us. Oh, Colin!"

Colin appeared at the doorway.

"Make about three carbons, Colin," said Charley. "We'll want some record of this transaction, too. Now jes' set at ease, Ed, and if you grab at this here check again I'll je'k a knot in your tail."

Colin came out on the verandah with the agreement and a fountain pen. "You can sign where you see your name typed," he said, thrusting them at the lawyer.

Semple licked his lips which were pallid and dry, but he signed.

Colin and Charley signed also and Semple was given one of the carbons. "I'll keep the original, Ed, jes' in case you was to ever take a notion to say what we had on the carbon wasn't what you had on the original."

"Why, Charley ... what a thing to say!"

"Well, goddammit, I said it. You kin git back to your boss and tell him fer me that he'll git a bill for every square inch of bark John Prince knocks off my standin' timber."

Semple wiped his fat perspiring face with a white linen handkerchief and treated his bald head to a similar operation. "I was instructed," he began with a noticeable lack of conviction, "to make some preliminary negotiations regarding extension of the lease which expires next month."

Charley nodded. "Yeah, I thought some such idea was in your head."

"It will be a magnificent gesture if you'll just let the lease extend in its present form. Think of the men that would be out of work if they had to shut the mills ..."

"You think of 'em," snapped Taradon sharply. "I ain't in business to run no relief agency no more'n Ben and the rest of 'em. If they was so all-fired good why don't they raise them starvation wages they're payin' in this here times of high prices?"

Colin said, "I can tell you right now what you'll get on your next lease, Mr. Semple. Culls. In other words, you'll cut not a single tree that has promise. There's plenty of good pulp trees on this tract. Enough to last for years. You'll cut culls in all sizes. Trees that won't amount to anything regardless of size you can cut. You can thin certain areas of even good trees as long as there is a Taradon forester breathing down your neck. Truck roads will be made according to certain specified conditions in the contract. There will be an assessment against damage and this will be made by our foresters and accepted and paid by your company. You will clean up and burn all debris and will avoid fire hazards of all sorts."

Mr. Semple was having trouble breathing. He grew purple. "B-b-but, dag nab it, Mr. Campbell, you know no company can operate like that. Why it would be idiotic to sign any such contract."

"Who'n hell ast you to sign it?" snapped Charley beaming with admiration for Colin's speech. "Who'n hell gives a damn if you sign it or not? You heard what the man said to take it or leave it and don't come back here with a pack of 'compromises.' They won't be no compromise."

Semple rose to his feet, his face set and ominous. "Charley, you're making a mistake. You know Miller, Roberts and Belding well enough to know they won't take something like this lying down."

"Don't make a sniff of a difference how they take it. You heard what my forester said and that's the way it'll be."

Semple bit his lip. "O.K., Charley. Don't say I didn't warn you. You're buckin' a powerful bunch of men." With that he placed his hat carefully on his head and walked down the path to his car.

"Well, the first gun is fired."

Donna came on the verandah. "But not the last one, you can bet. I think you're both stubborn fools."

"They framed Jack into a murder rap," snarled the old man. "Then they put the pressure on me to git that lease. What sort of a gran'daddy you think you got to take somethin' like that 'thout bitin' back?"

"But it's so hopeless. They'll either get Colin into a mess like they got Jack or they'll shoot both of you. Have you no sense at all?"

"Sense is not the thing right now," said Colin quietly. "I know how Charley feels and I feel the same way. What would the world come to if everyone took the easy way out?"

"You'd be alive ... which you might not be if you try to fight this thing," she said.

"*Who*," asked Colin, "wants to be alive and under foot?"

"There," exulted Charley pounding his stumps. "Who ... we asks you?"

CHAPTER FIVE

COLIN, WHO HAD worked in Washington with the forestry service and who had made friends in other departments, was expecting a letter from a friend in the Treasury Department, went to Silver River that afternoon to try to get the letter, only to find the Post Office closed.

Finding time on his hands he went to a baseball game where he was treated to an experience that he had not expected. The home pitcher was disabled by a hot liner through the box and had to leave the game making a collective groan go up from the home town rooters. This was stilled, then burst into a roar of approval as Donna, clad in a red jacket and blue pedal pushers, took his place and from there on allowed one scratch single from the next twelve batters who faced her. In addition to her superb performance on the mound she crossed up both the infield and the outfield by hitting late and poking a long rolling ball down the first base line and stretching it into a three bagger. She was batted home by Jeff Sessions the catcher who golfed a homer over the right field fence and came in with the winning run.

After the game, at the shower room where the jubilant team had gallantly given her first at the shower, Colin met her and almost hugged her in his joy.

"I didn't know you had it in you Chicken."

"There's a lot you don't know … Oh, Colin, I want you to meet Sturges Miller."

Ben Miller's son, he thought as he shook hands with the big young man whose dark curly hair lay flat on his well shaped head. He was handsome in a petulant sort of way and he seemed to be the sort of man who got his own way.

"Campbell … Oh, yes. The man who drives a hard contract." Miller's smile was personable and friendly.

Colin's lips moved from his teeth but it was not much of a smile. "Only one contract."

Miller lost interest in contracts as his eyes roved over Donna in a manner that made Colin's muscles grow taut.

"Tell Gramp I might be late, Colin. Sturges' bootlegger has a new vintage we're going to try out."

"I'll tell him," said Colin dryly.

Colin didn't like it and neither did Charley when he was told of the date with Sturges, but before they had much time to air their grievances the Dodge came up the drive and wheeled past the house to the garage.

"She come in early," said Charley spitting into the yard.

"I don't like that either," said Colin as he got up. "She went too straight and too fast to her own room." Colin got up nervously and walked back through the house to her bedroom, and knocked.

"Who is it?" Donna called.

"Colin. I want in."

"You can't come in—I'm not decent."

"Never mind your morals; let me in."

"Go away, Colin. I'm not letting you in." A cold fear smote him and he raised his voice. "You open this door or I'll kick it in. What's the matter with you?"

"I'm not going to open the door." Her voice broke and Colin took a step back and dealt the door a fearful blow with his foot.

The catch snapped and the door flew open to reveal a rather disheveled Donna with fingernail marks on her throat and a small but noticeable mouse under her left eye.

Colin advanced to where she sat before her mirror, looking forlorn and miserable. She was very close to tears.

"So, nothing's the matter? Well, what happened to you, run into a door?" he asked.

"Please let me alone, Colin. It's my own affair."

"That's what you think," he said raspily.

She turned around. "Please go. Nothing happened ..."

"With fingernail scratches on your neck and a black eye ..." He moved closer. "And your pants half torn off you but nothing's happened?" He clenched his teeth. "Was it Miller?"

Colin stood and looked at her for a long moment then whirled around. Charley hung like a great sloth to a rod near the door. "That's it, son, go git the son of a bitch." He bellowed, chinning himself with excitement.

Donna leaped to her feet and ran to the door. "Gramp, stop him."

The old man cackled gleefully. "Is you a plumb damn fool? Things is beginning to happen."

She turned about and dejectedly went back to her seat before the old dressing table. "I hope you are satisfied that they are."

"What happened, Honey?" asked her grandfather softly.

She threw her head back causing her soft hair to gleam like polished metal in the light. "Sturges got a little too amorous and when I slapped him he really got rough. That old glove compartment door fell open as usual and I clipped him over the knot with a crescent wrench. Then I took him to the Yellow Parrot and gave him to some of his drunken friends."

Charley eyed her for a while, hanging by one hand, absently scratching his belly with the other. "Don't 'pear to be upset much by it?"

"I'm not, that's why I tried to keep Colin from getting on his white horse."

"I ain't never been able to figger you out," he said, his eyes twin slits of concentration.

"Gramp, will you please close the door when you go, Colin broke the lock."

"What he shoulda done was wear you out where you're set-tin'." He slammed the door and swung away toward his own room.

Colin stopped the town marshal as he was walking sedately along the main street of Silver River. "Officer, where'd I most likely find Sturges Miller?"

The old man spat distastefully into the gutter and removed his black hat. "One place or t'other," he said scratching his bald head. "At home or that there dump, the Yaller Parrot."

"Where's the Parrot?"

"Go on down Main and turn right at the hotel. That'll put you on Osyka Street which'll cross the creek if you folly it fur enough. Parrot is on the east bank of the creek. Can't miss it."

Colin thanked him and shifted the jeep into high. When he entered the little bar and dance hall there were only a few couples about. Two teen agers who were drunkenly pawing each other, a boy almost on top of a little redhead who didn't appear over fifteen. He'd pull her dress up nearly to her waist, high enough to show her pink panties and she'd push his hand away and pull at her dress half heartedly. A man in blue overalls snored at a table where his last bottle of beer had overturned and now his face rested peacefully in the puddle. Sturges was slumped over the bar with both hands wrapped around a drink as though it would escape him. Colin, feeling a little nauseated, walked to the bar. He clamped a hard hand on the man's thick shoulder and twisted it about with enough power to almost unseat him.

"Goddamn it, you're 'bout t' buss m' shoulder," he complained drunkenly.

"Come outside, Miller. You have a date with a beating."

"No rough stuff in here, Mister," said the bar man glancing at his bung starter to see if it was readily available.

"That's why I asked him out," said Colin.

"W'l I be gardam," ejaculated Sturges peering at Colin owlishly. "Y'mean you wanna kig m'tail, brudda? W'y I'm so drung y' could kick me over with your foot." Sturges giggled at his remark. "Yezzir with your l'l tootsie y' could kig me right in a pile …" He took the last few drops from his drink. "S'Galahad, I din … dring a toast to y'. T' knight on the white horse and all the tin drawers and such ancient and honorable trappings." He put the glass on the bar. "Come on, Sir Galahad … jus's well get ma tail kigged an' go on home … ready?"

Colin sighed. "No. I don't fight drunks. I didn't realize you were that drunk."

"See," said Sturges to the bar man. "Tole you he was a knight of ole … won't take 'vantage of a drunk. Well, Sir Cam'ell, I probably couldn't fight my way out of a crepe shreep … suz … t' hell with it. I pick such odd things t' say … but don't think I'm 'fraid to take you on, brudda. Drung or sober, name y'r weapon and place an' I'll even give you a pair of kid gloves t' slap m' face with and y' don' need t' call me a poltroon. I awreddy know it but, son, sumbody sh-h-hould tell you a few things. Y'know that Donna is quite a gal, yessir, quite. Jump me on that, why don't you, Sir Cam'ell?"

The tightness went out of Colin's shoulders and he scrutinized the sweat-lined face of the drunken man. Oddly enough the wilfulness and weakness had disappeared and now there was only hatred and disgust and bitterness in evidence. Colin wondered at whom it was directed.

A little wail rose at the teen agers' table, punctuated with gasps which were halfhearted protests. Colin turned around to see one white slim leg on the table top and the other bare of dress extended to the floor, the muscles strutted and sharply defined.

"Hey you," called the bartender in a voice that was strident only to make it carry. "Take her out of here fer your fun."

The boy came to his feet and glared insolently. "O.K., Mister Wise guy ... Mister son of a bitch. Come on, Lissy ... where we can play in peace." The girl giggled and stood up, letting her dress fall in answer to gravity.

"Damn kids," muttered the bartender. "Give my place a bad name."

Sturges almost fell from the bar laughing. "We couln' let that happen, Otis ... s'shame." He turned to Colin. "Make you a bargain. You take me home and I'll tell you a few things I wouldn't if I wasn't drunk ... Bargain?"

Colin nodded. "Yes, I'll take you home."

Sturges stood carefully then grinned delightedly. "B'lieve I can make it, Sir Cam'ell, believe I can." He made it very well by using chairs, the walls and door facing. He went down the steps one at a time and started for the jeep. He reeled and caught himself against an old Chevrolet and straightened up. "Well ... whadder y'know."

As Colin came closer he could see the two bodies on the back seat locked in a tight ecstatic embrace, the little redhead's hair spread out on the back of the seat, her white face pinched and a dribble of saliva on her insufficient chin, her eyes tightly closed.

Her body moved sinuously and the little rodent-like whine came from her throat at every breath.

Colin grimaced. "Come on," he said roughly, catching the other by the arm.

Sturges frowned and pouted. "I wanted to see," he complained.

"I've seen enough," said Colin leading him to the jeep. "Now what was this you agreed to tell me?"

After lighting a limp cigarette with some difficulty he answered. "All up ina air 'bout Donna, eh … Well, put your hand up here fella."

Colin felt of the indicated spot and his fingers sank into a deep gash which was wet in the center and crusted with dried blood around the edges.

"She conked me … laid me out. That's your li'l Donna, son. I could show you certain other spots that she's contused and lac … er … cut, too. Now, son, lissen to your poppa. That gal jus' loves to be manhandled, then she'll get enough. Whether you got enough she don't care. You know about Jack … Well he treated her like dirt and used to beat her about a lot and she ate it up. Then one night Jack shoved her over on the bed for a li'l of his own kinda fun. Well, I don't know whether he made the grade or not but way after while she hauled off and conked him with her fist and knocked him cold. He was pretty drunk at the time so he wasn't hard to tap out. Yes, Sir Cam'ell, you could probably kick the hell out of me any day in the week … I heard what you did to John Prince and he's the cock of the walk in these parts. But what'd it get you?" Sturges seemed to get soberer as they drove slowly along the shadowy street. "Yeah, what'd it prove or improve or change?"

A succession of emotions had swept Colin while he listened and all the anger went out of him. Things seemed understandable now in full insofar as his knowledge went but what if she proved to be beyond his knowledge? He bit his lip and gripped the wheel of the jeep harder.

"You can't win either," said Sturges half to himself.

"Why do you say that?" Colin asked.

"Because I know what I'm talkin' about. You can't win. If it appears that you will win then you have lost for certain. Think I like all this crummy stinkin' double dealin'? Know what I took in school? I'm a qualified clinical psychologist and sociologist. I think along those lines and I'm impressed with what it all means but try to practice it. I tried to get Dad to pay his men a living wage and to fire that scum he has hanging about polluting the town. That kid you saw all locked up in the back of that car was John Prince's youngest daughter. The oldest died of septicemia after a rotten butchery of an abortion; the next in line has a child—a stunted wailing wormy-brained monstrosity and she isn't a lot better. She went from a hundred and forty pounds to ninety. She's an agate-eyed wreck, her mother stays drunk all the time and he lives with a Negro slut out in the woods whose own people won't have anything to do with her. That's the kind of people that my father and his precious partners hire. The boy you saw is the son of the high school principal and if he doesn't get himself a dose tonight it'll be through divine intervention. What a salutary effect this all is having on the town. Rotten and getting more so ... Hold it ..."

Colin stopped the car and let Miller vomit, feeling that a similar operation might relieve him also but manfully held it back.

Sturges wiped his mouth with his handkerchief, then mopped his face and forehead from which ran rivulets of cold sweat. He lay back and breathed deeply. "Know what my title is ... Supervisor of Personnel Welfare ... grooming me to the sufficiently comatose position of a crown prince who will one day inherit the empire ... and I haven't got the guts to do anything but conform. Cam'bell … goddammit, you have a first name, don't you?"

"Yes, you can call me Colin."

"Well, Colin, what do you think of a man who knows better, whose very guts are being shredded to pieces by this maggoty setup and hasn't two cents' worth of spark to do anything about it?"

Colin turned a corner and took off on a little narrow country road. He wasn't ready to take his passenger home yet. "I think this … and listen to what I have to say. You're sticking because you have an unconscious conviction that in some fashion, in some way, you're going to be able to do some good. You're drinking yourself to death because your conscious mind in all logic cannot see any way to accomplish this. *Isn't that true?*"

The effect of his last sentence drove Sturges upright in his seat. He stared at Colin for a while then hid his face in his hands and wept like a horribly beaten child. Colin let him storm it out of his system without saying a word. The paroxysm finally abated and Sturges blew his nose and sat straighter in his seat.

"I made fun of you a while ago," he said quietly, his throat jerking spasmodically a couple of times. "I'm bitterly, abjectly sorry. I'm so ashamed of myself that I could puke from sheer self-energizing nausea. The more I talk the worse it sounds … I'm shutting up."

Colin struck him a hard blow on the shoulder with his open hand. "Cut it out. If you're a psychologist you know the value of talk. You've had a good cleansing and I know you feel better. If you think you're beaten then you are beaten and you'll get further and further into the mire of alcohol and self-disgust, so why not snap out of it and climb on the band wagon?"

"You mean the bone wagon. You can't buck it, Colin … haven't you heard what happened to Jack?"

Colin nodded. "Yes, and that's one reason why I'm here. There's a girl, a girl who is all mixed up, terribly unhappy, terribly ashamed of herself but who still can't help what she is, or I should say will be if she continues the way she's been going. There's an old man who has no legs but who, in spite of it, has managed to make a go of it, manage his plantations and can still laugh and be amusing. There's a hundred thousand acres of the most beautiful land ever put on earth, trees by the million, wild life, clean, cool air unpolluted by smoke and foul vapors from close packed humanity. There are cold clear streams that will become muddy little highways for top soil to go down to the ocean and be lost if this land is raped and pillaged. I won't be stopped by the Miller, Roberts, Belding combine. I won't be stopped by rotten politics and the only thing they *can* do is to kill me."

"And what makes you think they won't?" Sturges asked.

"I don't know. Maybe it's the sort of thing that kept Columbus going in the face of storm, water shortage, unseen monsters and mutiny."

Sturges was silent for a long while. He sighed heavily, gagged a little, and lit another cigarette. "You know I'm as big a man as you, in avoirdupois. In another way I'm not even a speck on this seat. It's a wonder you can see me and even more so that you'll sit here and listen to me weep, wail and gnash my teeth over what a washout I am."

"Let's make up our mind," said Collin. He pulled the jeep over to the side of the road and stopped. "Are you a washout or are you just a man with no sense of direction? If it's the latter, get aboard with some who do have a little direction and you won't have to duck every morning when you shave. Stay the way you are and you'll wind up at Jackson in a ward for incurable alcoholics. You'll be beaten and crucified because you know what's right and you can't scrape up the courage to do something about it.

Old Charley and I intend to whip this thing to a standstill and if we don't we'll take whatever comes. In losing a fight there is a certain satisfaction if you've given it all you had, and if you don't you still have to live with yourself ..."

"Don't tell me that," flared the other. "Don't I know? I'm now faced with knuckling under and learning all the tricks of backbiting, scrounging, and the impeccable dishonesty which is the stock in trade of line politicians. You know—kiss the babies, ruin the men if they don't cleave to the line, spread gossip where it'll do the most good, or harm depending on where you're sitting, frame, beat, bribe, trade, Jesus! ... and they talk about a relatively clean gang massacre as though it was something reprehensible when as a rule they only murder other gangsters from whom some politician has withdrawn protection."

"You talk pretty," snarled Colin, "but where are you sitting? Are you snapping in for the booby hatch or standing up like a man and doing something glorious if foolish?"

Sturges flung his cigarette away with a savage gesture. "Do you realize what it would mean for me to break with Dad?"

"Sure, probably better than you do. You also know what it'll mean not to. Take your choice and take it now because in the event that you decide to stand up on your own two feet for a change we've some things to talk over. Otherwise, you go home and try to sleep with yourself."

Sturges yanked cruelly at his hair in an agony of indecision. Could he throw everything out of the window—family, career, friends ... friends? Not those people his father had been shoving him in contact with whose interests lay in cultivating and fawning for reasons of their own. "Okay, brother, you've bought yourself an ally with a line of hard language which happens to be true. You're right at every turn and all I have to fight your logic with is a hank or so of worn out implied loyalty which I've never felt and despise in every nerve I've got. What do I do?"

Colin shuddered deep inside. A great weight dropped from him and he breathed freely for the first time in an hour. "You do exactly nothing till you see something to do, then you do it to the best of your ability and reason. You are in a good position to help because you're on the inside. You know the hazards of the game and we can only guess them. You know what they might do and again we can only guess. If you can just keep us a little ahead of them and let us prepare for possible contingencies. Tell me, do they have a real good ace in the hole?"

Sturges shrugged. "What do they need with an ace in the hole when they have the judge, the sheriff, and all the patronage for the district and innumerable men dependent on them for a living?"

Colin bit his lip. "There's one thing I've been thinking about. I know of the night that Jack and Donna had the set to. A Negro saw a part of it. He ran!"

Miller's face turned ghastly in the moonlight. "You mean you think ..."

"Yes, that's what I think. She's all the old man has now and she's his most vulnerable spot. If they got a picture like that of her and Jack, then they're in the saddle and no mistake. I'm afraid of what would happen if they ever showed it to him and I have an idea they won't. To me more likely, knowing that to show it to him might cause an explosion but if I saw it and understood just what it would mean I'd either pull in my horns or I'd ... Hell, I don't know."

Sturges quivered like a sick man in a cold draft. "Jesus, but I need a drink."

"Do you know of any such thing?"

"You mean the picture?"

"Yes."

"No, I don't, but that doesn't mean there isn't one. I think the old man would keep something like that from me until I get a few more layers of scar tissue. I'm sort of tender yet."

"Well, do what you can as you see it. We don't have much to go on and anything you can smell out will be welcome."

Sturges nodded. "I'll do the best I can but don't expect too much. You'd better take me home now."

CHAPTER SIX

THE NEXT MORNING Colin sat at breakfast with a strange chill around his heart. In spite of his education and enormous reading of books relating to human action and reaction he felt a touch of disappointment in regard to Donna. What *was* she, after all? What did it matter to him? He ducked the question with a swiftness which should have indicated something, and had someone else done so he would have caught it immediately. He looked at her as she sat quietly eating her eggs and ham. Her eye was still a little purple and the scratches were still on her neck, otherwise she seemed all right. If the occasion had left any mental disturbance it wasn't obvious.

After breakfast she cornered him in the hall. "What did you do to Sturges last night?"

He eyed her steadily. "Nothing," he said slowly.

She looked away. "I'm glad … you see, it wasn't all his fault."

"That's what he told me."

"He did?"

"Yes. He said it wasn't the first scar you had put on him."

"Yes," she whispered. "Now you hate me, don't you?"

"Would that make any difference?"

"It would make a great deal of difference." Her voice was warm and ineffably soft but he forced it past his immediate attention.

"Then, why do you do it Donna?"

She hung her head and two big tears rolled down her cheeks. "Please don't ask me that!"

He patted her on the shoulder. "I'm sorry. Forget I asked it."

He turned and went to the kitchen porch where Charley hung by one hand giving orders to Willie. "Joe Stratton is bringing that buckskin mare over today to breed to King. He'll be here 'fore dinner, so … Hi, bub. What's on fer today?"

"Didn't you say last night that you couldn't get George on the phone?"

"Yap. I guess he's shinin' up to some nigger gal or watchin' John Prince."

"Did he ever bring in those checks?"

"No. He's got 'em though. I talked to him the next day. He was supposed to bring 'em in yestiddy mornin' but I guess he had somethin' else to do."

"I'm going up there to see what the holdup is. Those checks should be here and well hidden. We might need them."

"What fer? We got paid fer the timber. Paid pretty well, too."

"Not for the timber but for the evidence that they deliberately tried to steal the timber. It's very well to lay it all on John Prince but you know that's a lie. Somewhere along the line—if we can make Prince talk—he might tell us some more about it."

"Okay, go ahead. Tell George to keep an eye open and report any funny doin's; but he'll do that anyhow. Want me to go along?"

"Not necessary, unless you want to."

"Uh huh. She's gonna be a scorcher today and it'll rain this evenin'. I'll stay here and plot."

Colin pulled the jeep over under a thick-leafed gum tree and crawled slowly out. There was no sign of life near the tower nor about the little cabin which housed the ranger assigned to the area. Colin stopped suddenly. His spine tingled and his muscles grew taut. Something was wrong because the jeep George used was in its place under the little shed beside the cabin. Warily he walked toward the cabin, his eyes searching the brush that grew around the edge of the little clearing where the cabin and tower were. Colin stopped and gazed upward examining the galvanized length of the steel lattice work. Nothing seemed amiss till he noticed the hanging telephone wire. It had broken about halfway between the nearest post and the top of the tower. The piece still attached to the tower was as straight as a ruler showing that whatever broke it stretched the wire to the limit of its tensile strength before breaking it.

Following the pointing wire to the ground Colin drew a sharp breath. With a spring he bounded back to the jeep and took a well worn but well kept .45 automatic from the seat. He unwrapped layers of stockinette from the weapon and worked a cartridge into the chamber. Then he walked over toward a still figure half hidden in the grass. Swarms of blue bottle flies arose in humming protest as Colin approached. The man was dead without a doubt, his neck twisted queerly, his face out of sight in the grass. With a grimace he turned the body over. It was not George. Colin stood for some time looking down at the body. He massaged his chin meditatively and catching a whiff of the body which though not yet acrid carrion was still a sickening sweetish reek that made the muscles of his nose twitch involuntarily. He turned away and approached the shanty. The door was not quite shut and he moved it inward with the toe of his shoe. On his bunk lay George, his head propped up and his eyes open. "Hi," he whispered. "Didn't think you'd ever git here."

"What happened," asked Colin.

George shrugged. "Search me … that's what they did. Lookin' fer them checks and they got 'em."

"Who's the man dead outside?" Colin asked.

George's eyes went wide and he attempted to sit up but was too weak. "I don't know ... God a'mighty. I wonder if it's Jesse? He was supposed to come over ..."

"Is Jesse a little squatty man with a bald head?"

George swallowed noisily and nodded.

"Then it's him. Looks like he was thrown or fell from the tower."

George shuddered. "They musta got me first and he come and went to lookin' fer me and went up in the tower. They musta been up there lookin' fer the checks. I hid 'em in a little crack just over the phone. I woke up later and tried to call y'all but the line was dead. I come to the bunk to sorta ketch up some stren'th and I guess I passed out. I musta lost a gallon of blood."

"They shoot you?"

"Yair. In the shoulder. I guess they thought they had killed me but they didn't. I gotta git outa here, Mr. Campbell, and git to a doc. I woke up early this mornin' burnin' up ..."

"Sure, George. I guess I'm just bowled over. I'll fix that line and call in for an ambulance."

It took Colin just ten minutes to splice the wire and call Charley. The old man exploded in lurid profanity. "I'll git the ambylance and I'll call the sheriff. That'll be the thing to watch close, son. Call Toby Acker frum station five to come over. Toby is a pretty sharp ole duck."

Three hours later Toby Acker showed up. "Whut 'nell's going on 'roun' here?"

Toby wouldn't weigh over a hundred pounds, had no teeth, a sharp nose and chin. Tobacco juice stained the corners of his mouth and freckled the front of his faded blue shirt. He hitched up trousers that were too big for him and walked over to peer long and intently at the corpse, muttering to himself all the time. Then he walked over to the tower and began to climb the ladder.

Colin followed and arrived at the top sweating and winded. Toby wasn't even breathing very hard. Together they looked the place over carefully but being only a small cubicle with little floor space there wasn't much looking to do.

"I've been up here once," offered Colin. I didn't see a thing. The checks are gone, though." He pointed to the crack over the telephone.

Toby spat accurately out into space and continued his search. "Hummmm. Umhummm."

"Find something?"

"Mebby so, mebby not ... look here." On the sill of the west window were smudges and four long furrows.

"Could he have fallen?" asked Colin.

Toby uttered a vulgar four-lettered word. "Fall? Jesse Fallon fall outa one o' these things?"

He used the word again and spat a small caliber stream through the window. "Could you fall outa here?"

"I don't think so."

"Y' know damn well y' couldn't. He didn't fall neither. Come on, I want to look at sumpn'."

Toby led the way down the ladder and approached the body again. He looked at the fingernails of the left hand very carefully, then the right. He grunted, "Looky here."

Colin looked. The nails were full of gray paint such as the tower was painted with.

"Fell, huh?" asked Toby with stinging sarcasm.

Colin shook his head. "I didn't think so at first."

Toby straightened up. "Well, ain't nothin' we c'n do. Here comes the law. Now for some fas' brain work, the potgutted son of a wolf bitch cow."

Sheriff Potter climbed importantly from his Lincoln coupe followed by a deputy. A Ford sedan painted a bright red and marked "SHERIFF" pulled up behind and disgorged four more deputies.

"They musta heered the' was a massacree," suggested Toby ejecting his cud, allowing it to fall with a moist plop on the ground.

"Evenin', boys," said Potter pompously as he waddled up. He was short with a girth of some fifty-four inches and had a habit of pulling up his trousers with one hand and fingering himself in the inguinals with the other. His face was placid and utterly expressionless, his eyes peering with some difficulty, it appeared, out of dungeons of suet. His posture had that turkey-strutted erectness seen in fat men who either hold themselves thus or fall on their faces.

"What's come off here?" he asked, waddling up closer and peering at the body.

"It appears that someone threw Fallon from the tower," offered Colin.

"Well now," breathed Potter aghast. "Who'd do a thing like that?"

"Been rumored," said Toby caustically, "that the county's payin' you to find out just that."

Potter beamed like Toby had paid him a compliment. "Well, you know that's a fact, ain't it?"

"Hit air," snapped Toby.

Colin explained what he had found and told him about George being shot and that they had sent him in to Silver River hospital.

"Beats all," said Potter with his expression of mild incredulity. "I sorta wish though that you hadn't moved him till I arrived."

"How come?" asked Toby. "Want another stiff on your hands?"

"Oh, no, indeed. I didn't mean that. What I meant is …"

"Sounded almighty like it to me," said Toby who turned his back and worried a chew from a plug of B. F. Gravely's Superior. Potter stared at the little man's back with mild disapproval.

"I don't think Toby approves of me," he said complainingly to Colin.

He turned to the deputy who had driven the Lincoln and another who came in the Ford. "Joe, you and Dick run up the tower and have a look. Look sharp now. I'm a little too plump," he said to Colin apologetically.

Colin pointed to the wire which he had repaired and told him how he had found it. "I feel sure the body broke the wire and I wouldn't have touched it except that I had to get some help for George."

The sheriff tut-tutted and made other noises with his mouth. "I wish you hadn't bothered that wire but I can appreciate why you did it. It ain't good to be way out with a hurt man on your hands."

The men came down from the tower after a ten-minute search. "Don't find a thing, Sheriff," said Dick. "Guess he fell out."

Potter tut-tutted some more and sighed heavily. "Okay, boys. Load him in the trailer and we'll take him in."

"Jes' a minute," Toby's voice cracked with the force of his utterance. They turned and looked at him. "You mean t' tell me this here is a investigation?"

The sheriff looked pained. "Why, Toby, there ain't anything to investigate. He fell from the tower and ..."

"And I guess George shot hisself?"

Potter shrugged heavily. "I don't know ... did he?"

Toby's eyes glittered. "That's fine ... Jes' fine but when it gets around that yore investigation didn't show them fingernail scratches on that window sill up there and didn't show that there was paint of the same color under Jesse's nails and didn't show

69

that it's might' nigh unpossible fer a man t' fall outa that tower then you kin bet a lot of other talk is gonna git started. I'm gonna see to it."

"I wouldn't do that if I was you, Toby," said the sheriff mildly. "Okay, boys, put him on the trailer."

Colin was speechless with rage. "Isn't it proper procedure for the coroner to pass on a few things before a man is moved?"

"Why no, not 'less I say so, son."

"Then allow me to compliment you on your utter and complete stupidity. One man dead and another shot and you gabble about falling out of a tower that a three-year-old couldn't fall from. Toby's right. We'll see to it that this get's nosed about."

Potter sighed again. "Son, that wouldn't do no good and it might start a ruckus."

"That's the idea," said Colin savagely. "We might even find out why you're so anxious to have this appear accidental."

Colin could see the mercilessness behind the sheriff's beady opaque eyes. "That's right, you might."

When they had left Colin cursed till his breath was gone but Toby merely looked around quietly. "Jes' whut I 'spected," he grumbled. "No need to git het up."

Colin walked over to the cabin and inspected the puddle of blood to the right of the steps where George had lain for a hour after being shot.

"Come over here, Toby. Now, I'm a little taller than George and I'm going to turn my back to the cabin. George was shot about here." He touched his chest high up on the right side. "Now take off about two inches and make an imaginary circle on the logs of the cabin with this spot as a center and about a foot wide."

Toby did better than that. He took a carpenter's pencil and drew a rough circle.

"Now," said Colin, "let's find that bullet. It went through George, clean." After a five-minute search with Toby probing the rough bark with his knife blade he found the hole. "Got it," he said exultantly.

"Hold it, Toby—can you feel the metal?"

"Right there at the end of the blade. It musta keyholed. You kin see that there wide hole."

"Get George's hand axe so we can take it out in a chip. Then we'll take it home chip and all. If we can ever use it we'll have it in the chip and the chip'll fit this cut here."

Toby grinned toothlessly. "You ain't so dumb, is you?" He went into the cabin and returned with the axe. "Better let me do it, bub," he said confidently. "I 'spect I done whacked out a lot more chips 'n you in my time."

He proved his contention and the chip flew out, cut perfectly and Colin put it in his pocket.

"I guess you can go on back to your station, Toby. You got a gun?"

Toby glanced at the handle of the .45 sticking out of Colin's shirt. "The sheriff didn't see that," he chuckled. "He couldn't see a winder open in a barn in the moonlight. Yair, I got a ole .45 Russian thumbcock Colt. I shot at a 'possum one night and knocked the corner block out frum under my corn crib."

Colin grinned tightly. "Then you'd better keep it handy. Don't bother to spy on John Prince. I'll keep an eye on him from the air. That might be why George got shot."

Toby nodded and walked over where he had hitched his red saddle mule. Colin climbed in the jeep and started back to the house.

At supper that night he almost ate himself sick. Having missed dinner he tried to make up for it. Charley sat morose and silent, picking pettishly at his food.

"Fell huh? Why that clabber-headed son of a bitch. What sort of a explanation did he have fer George gettin' shot?"

"None," mumbled Colin with his mouth full. "Toby cut the bullet out of the cabin and I brought it back in a chip that'll fit where it was cut from."

"I wonder who'll be next," murmured Donna half to herself.

Charley glared at her but said nothing. Colin continued to eat. After supper they went as usual out on the verandah to try to find a breeze. A faint zephyr blew from the east where heat lightning played fitfully along the horizon.

"Charley, did it ever occur to you that Semple had some other axe to grind by giving us that fat check?" asked Colin.

"Yair ... 'specially when he tried to snatch it 'way frum me. That's why I had you to type that long-winded receipt. Fer one thing, I think he wanted them cancelled checks back and maybe he wanted to say we agreed to sumpn' else."

"Yes, that's what I have been thinking about but it doesn't seem logical that they'd try anything like that with a contract renewal coming up."

"Humans ain't logical. Them three men tries to figger a long time ahead and we sits here and tries to logic out whut they're meanin' by some move close around. It won't work out that way. We gotta try to be ready fer *whatever* happens and too much thinkin' won't he'p much. Might even make us study up some wrong move or git ourselves bound up in some opinion. Since we're lettin' them take the lead then we can't 'spect to stay ahead of 'em. All we can do is be ready."

"Yes, I suppose you're right," admitted Colin regretfully. "However, we have a man in the enemy camp."

"Who, that codger? Well, I wouldn't put too much expect on him 'cause he ain't in a position to know too much even if he is a willin' little cuss."

"No, I mean Sturges."

Charley uttered a violent word. "You mean the boy?"

"Yes, I had a long talk with him last night."

"Th' hell you did. I thought you left here to whale hell outa him?"

Colin felt his face getting hot. "Well, that is, I … I did, but he was too drunk to do anything to him."

Charley grunted. "How'd you make a deal with a drunk man?"

"I rode him around till he got sober. The boy is all cut up inside because of his dad's methods and policies. Seems they're trying to groom him for a spot in the organization. He might be able to help us."

"How do you know he ain't one o' them Trojan horses I read about once?"

Colin shook his head. "You'll have to take my judgment there. He was drunk when I first saw him and I think he was being sincere."

Charley grumbled and swung back into his chair. "Well, whut we got 'cept a bullet in a chip from Number Four tower cabin, a shot man, a dead one and a goddam eggheaded sheriff?"

Colin smiled ruefully. "That's about all, right now. I got a letter from an Internal Revenue pal of mine in Washington today and as far as they can tell Ben, Robert's and Belding's income tax is all right. I was hoping we could work something from that end."

"To smart fer that," muttered Charley. "They're beatin' it but we ain't got a chanct to show how."

"Maybe somethin'll break for us. I'll make some inquiries and I'll set Sturges to looking at that angle. That colored boy might even be of some help. We'll see."

Charley grunted pessimistically and swung up on his trapeze. "I'm sayin' good night. See y'all in the mornin'."

Donna took possession of Charley's chair as soon as he disappeared through the hall door. "What terrible things are you thinking about me, Colin?"

He touched her hand gently. "I'm not …"

"Don't touch me." Her voice was harsh and strained. "Oh, Colin, I didn't mean it that way," as he took his hand back quickly. "You're being kind to me and it makes me go all soft and quivery inside. Please don't be kind to me and gentle—I'll just cave in like melting ice cream if you do."

"As I started to say," he murmured gently. "I'm not thinking any sort of terrible things about you because I think I know enough about you to realize why you are like that."

She hid her face in her hands. "I *hate* me!"

"And that's the worst thing you could possibly do. Remorse is a disease, an illness," he said.

"Are you being perfectly honest with me?"

"I've never been anything else."

She wiped tears from her eyes with a man's pocket handkerchief. "Yes, I know that and I've behaved terribly toward you."

"I wish you wouldn't bother about that. I've told you I understood and you don't have to beat yourself to pieces because of what has gone on before."

She remained silent for a few minutes. "You were so right the other night that I thought someone had told you about me. I hated you for a while then I realized that you must really see what you told me from your own intelligence. I'm bitterly sorry, Colin, I really am."

He took her hand, this time by main force. "Donna, if you'd only stop punishing yourself. It's all right. I intended nothing but to show you that I knew something about you so you'd let up and talk to me and you can see it has worked."

She squeezed his hand convulsively. "Knowing me as you do I don't see how you can be so kind?"

He shook her shoulder. "Because I'm a softie at heart," he said lightly. "I dislike seeing anyone unhappy. I despise it, I'm revolted at it, I fight it … too zealously sometimes, nevertheless I continue to fight."

A sob seemed to catch in her throat and shake her like a hiccough. "I carried on so awfully with Jack. He never had the manhood in him to be anything but what he was and I knew it, yet when the chips were down I'm afraid I caved in a little too readily."

"Whatever happened between you and Jack," said Colin steadily, "is past. You were very, very young and you were in love with him or thought you were."

"But I could have fought him off … I should have fought him off." Tears flowed freely and shimmered like subdued topazes on her cheeks.

Colin caught her shoulders and turned her around to face him. "Look here. Whatever you did that night is past—done with."

True to her prediction Donna crumpled forward and wept with hard stormy bitterness. For a long time she rested her head on his arms and nature performed one of her cleansing miracles. She slipped from her chair to her knees and buried her face in his lap, clutching his thighs with desperate convulsiveness. He placed a big arm across her shoulders, squeezed her hard but said nothing.

Sometime later she raised her head. "See," she quavered, "I told you."

He took her face in his hands, his heart pounding hard in his chest. "So what?" he said softly, "I've wanted to see you do that ever since I came here. I'll bet you feel like a million."

She nodded, her amethyst eyes, bright and wet, studying the rugged angular lines of his face. "Colin!"

"Yes?"

"For a big man you're so much like a mother."

He turned her face up and gently kissed her damp salty lips with such infinite tenderness that it produced a sharp longing pain under her heart. Then he drew back. "And you, poor child, you've needed a mother for so long, haven't you?"

"Oh, Colin, if you only knew ... but you do know of course. That's why you're like you are."

He stood up drawing her with him. "I won't be content to remain a mother, though," he told her lightly and kissed her again, quickly, fleetingly "It's bedtime for you," he added.

She looked at him closely for a long moment and nodded.

Colin undressed to his shorts without turning on the lights and lay on top of the bed relaxed, listening to the night sounds and the rustle of a camellia bush not too far from his window. A light cool breeze had sprung up and magically dissipated the heat. His skin was cool from his shower and he was sleepily seeking the buttons of his shorts when he realized with something like prescience that he was not alone in the room. She stood by the door in web thin pajamas watching him quietly.

He sat up on the edge of the bed. "Is there something wrong, Honey?" he asked, unconsciously using Charley's term of endearment.

She ran to him and fell on her knees, resting her face on his bare leg. The contact of her soft cool skin sent a high voltage ripple through him. "I tried to stay away, Colin ... God help me, I tried. I just couldn't. Take me to the door and throw me out—make me leave you."

Colin was debating just such a move when suddenly the realization struck him that some powerful urge must have made her enter his room. A compulsion so powerful that to deny it and forcibly make her leave might do untold harm. If he allowed her to stay he knew what would happen, but he felt better capable of making it right with her this way than if he ran the risk of hurting her intolerably by making her leave the room.

He stood up and lifted her easily in his powerful arms. The touch of her thin clothing made his skin crawl with rapture and the hard-softness of her luxurious body beneath was like a draught of strong drink that made his nerves harden and quiver. He didn't kiss her at first; he just held her close allowing the warmth of their bodies to mingle, fitting with firm insistence from knees to chest, savoring the touch with sheer animal ecstasy. The pointed hardness of her high breasts stung his skin like twin electrodes and his muscles responded involuntarily.

He filled both hands with her thick soft hair forcing it back over her shoulders, then slowly he bent and kissed her parted lips which mingled softly and unresistingly with his. He twisted her around till she was resting in the crook of his right arm, her own arms encircling his neck where they clung with hard demanding strength. The top of her questing tongue touched the highly sensitive under surface of his lips, almost making him cry out.

He broke the contact with a gasp that was something frenzied, something fearful, but she dropped her arms beneath his and held him like bands of steel. His hand went beneath the flimsy pajama coat and caressed the length of her strong smooth back with its deep muscular trench, bringing them around under her armpits to seek the firm rise of her breasts. She drew breath with painful sharpness and slipped out of her pajama coat, flinging it to the floor and Colin picked her up and placed her on the bed.

He lay beside her, his searching lips caressing her till every part of her stood like early spikes of hyacinth, her breath coming in hard short gasps and her body moving restlessly from side to side. The body long contact of her was of such thunderous wonder that Colin almost swooned, but his hand moving almost of its own volition roved past her small waist and down her strong thighs. Her body twisted with a convulsive heave, tiny bubbles of sound forcing themselves past her back drawn lips.

She lay beside him on the bed, her long generous figure revealed by the glow of the stars and moon that filtered through the big windows. Her eyes were closed and her breath gentle and regular. Colin gazed at her with something akin to awe and reverence. What a cataclysmic thing it had been, her demands delivered with such terrific passion and strength that he felt winded and beaten. He hated to disturb her because now would come remorse but she couldn't stay there all night. He reached over and cupped one full breast in his hand. Instantly hers closed over his, forced it down hard. Her eyes opened and considered him with shadowy earnestness.

When she spoke her voice was tiny, childlike, and begging. "Do you hate me, Colin?"

He grinned widely hoping that she could see in the semi-darkness. Evidently she could because she rolled over into his embrace and sobbed softly on his great shoulder, her hand touching his face with adoring caress. Again hot blood flooded over him as her body touched him, and though he strove to think of other things the thundering pulse in his ears told of the uselessness of it. With rough brutal force he drew her to him, her eyes seeking his and her body thrusting hard against him. He kissed her long with finesse and finality, turning her till she lay flat on the bed.

CHAPTER SEVEN

Dawn was graying the eastern skies when Colin awoke. With a start that bounced him inches off the bed he glanced at the space beside him. It was empty and he relaxed, grinning ruefully at his start. He rolled over and the next sound he heard was an hour later from Willie.

"Bettuh git up from deh and drink dis hyer coffee fo' hit gits cole."

"I don't get any better," she told him with stricken sadness after breakfast in a shadowy corner of the hall. "It's not often but when it comes over me, Colin, I ..." Her throat worked as her voice choked off.

He took her face in his hands. "Listen to me, Honey. There has never been a night in my life like last night and there never will be again. There will be beauty again and again but last night was something special. It just can't be equaled. You were pure divinity. You were out of this world and what happened will go down in the books for all time as the most wonderful thing that ever happened to me. I feel that way, how can you feel so terrible?"

"Then you don't think I'm dirty or bad or evil or ..." Her words rushed out but stopped suddenly.

"Were you alone last night? Don't I get any credit or responsibility and don't you see what was proved?"

She shook her head looking at him tremulously.

"It was proved last night that you are as normal as anyone. Tough, rough, and super appetite if you will, but just as normal as the desire for a stomach full of food. Last night you were cleansed, relieved, and a very vulnerable little girl. You got overwhelmed by a lot of things and your nature just led you to my door and I'm grateful ... I'm glad it did."

She rested her head on his chest and cried silently for a while. "Colin, please believe me, Jack was the only one till you ... I guess the situation was similar but those times with Sturges we just fought and wrestled around. It wasn't the real thing. It seems I like to be brutalized ... hurt."

"Nothing like that happened last night, Honey," he reminded her. "That's why I say you're normal. There would have been no success otherwise."

She smiled a little and leaned over. He could see two purple spots at the base of her neck. There were two more on her arms where his powerful fingers had left their marks. "I have other marks, too," she said shyly.

Colin laughed. "In that case I guess we're pretty well met. I feel like I've been beaten with a hickory club. There's still nothing abnormal about it."

Donna flushed a bright red. "The way we discuss it here so freely it's a wonder ..." She broke off and looked away.

"My reasons are simple enough," he said. "I'm not ashamed of it."

Her eyes misted over and her throat throbbed. "Was there ever a man like you before in the whole world? You sooth me but I'm mixed up worse than ever now."

He grinned engagingly. "That's because you are at war with your background—you're wrestling with your conscience. Unless your conscience is a fellow traveler with the tyranny of your nature then it confuses you. Get 'em together." He bent swiftly and kissed her. "Chin up, chest out, caddy on and all that sort of rot." He turned away and went in search of Charley who sat on the verandah spitting thoughtfully in the yard.

"Call frum Potter this mornin'."

"Yeah! What'd he have to say."

"Said he was sorry 'bout Jesse 'n' George but wasn't nuthin' could do. No evidence."

"He still toying with the idea that George shot himself?"

"Nope, but he ain't tyin' Jesse in with George. Still says Jesse fell. Toby brung sumpn' in." Charley fumbled in his pockets and brought forth a bright brass cylinder.

Colin took it and looked at the base. "Denver Arsenal ... '43. Hummm, that's a thirty-calibre military cartridge. Wonder who has Army rifles around here?"

"I got one .45-70 Spanish American War Springfield ...'

"If that old blunderbuss had hit George it would have torn the arm off him. We can't use you this time. I think I'll look at the bullet." He went to his room and brought back the chip holding the bullet and began to carefully scrape the bark and wood away from the bullet. He stopped and looked hard at Charley. "Where'd Toby find this empty?"

"Mighty near a half mile away on that hill across from the tower. He rid his mule back thataway and seen it shinin' in the grass. Whoever done it wasn't no slouch of a shot."

Colin rubbed his chin and thought aloud. "Thirty-calibre ... Army rifle or sporting rifle using service ammo. Likely with a telescope sight. Good shot. That ought to narrow it down some." He got up and went into the hall and called Silver Creek. "Mr. Sturges Miller, please," he said in a gruff voice, to the man who answered the phone. "Speaking," said the voice.

"Mixit good," said Colin crisply and rapidly. "Info miles per hour re keen eyed pea plunker with G.I. tube, likely magnific eyeglass. Catch and Roger?"

"C 'n R," came the answer and the phone hung up quickly.

"What sorta monkey talk was that?" asked Charley glaring as Colin came back to the porch.

"G.I. gobbledgook," said Colin. "We used to foul it up like that to fool any listeners. That wasn't too good because I'm out of practice."

Charley grunted and spat. "Whatcha doin' today?"

"I think I'll snoop a little where Prince is cutting. I told Toby to stay away from him."

"Good idear. Don't want no more casualties and that means you, too."

"I'll keep it safe," said Colin indifferently.

"You ain't got idear of keepin' it safe," said Charley caustically. "You gonna git in trouble and mark my words. Remember, I ain't no sprig to go chasin' 'round rescuin' you."

"I hope it won't be necessary," said Colin, "but in the event I don't come back some day get word to Sturges. He's my boy."

"I hope so, but I don't trust none of that crowd."

"That's it—he *isn't* one of the crowd. He has tried to be and they've tried to make him but it's another case of conscience and education taking over."

Taking Willie, who by now was a renowned flyer, Colin flew over the area where Prince was supposed to be cutting but could locate no activity. No trucks, no men, and only a few signs since their last visit.

"What do you make of that," he yelled in Willie's ear.

Willie shrugged and shook his head. "Mebby dey on a vacation."

Colin flew home and landed but was far from satisfied. A call to Toby elicited information he didn't already know so he got in his jeep and rode out to the deserted tower. All was quiet in a sylvan way with the only sounds those of leaves rustling, insects scraping and the occasional cry of a bird. Again Colin had the feeling that things were not right and the skin at the back of his neck tightened. He got out and walked around stiff and wary but only the bark of a big fox squirrel was his reward. He crossed the creek again and headed toward the site of the last cutting. Still no sign of any activity.

Colin made a wide circle to the north and west through hills and valleys of beautiful second growth pine and scrub oak with the inevitable patches of seeder pines rearing their lofty heads high over the surrounding trees in austere and majestic contempt. He stopped under the cool branches for a while to take a smoke and relax. The feeling of alarm had vanished and now he was just hot and tired. The going had been devious and rough so he put his feet out of the side of the vehicle and stretched. The heady tang of wood smoke brought him erect with a sudden shin cracking lurch. He leaped out and stood erect sniffing and gauging the wind then leaping back to the wheel he tore off, careening dizzily between the great boles of the seeder trees, and suddenly he braked down hard.

In the very center of the grove stood a neat little house and from its bent kitchen stovepipe came the smoke he had smelled. Children began to appear in swarms till there were some dozen peering at him from various points of not too exposed vantage. He got out and savored the tidy little house and its domesticity. The children were stepped up from two to what he thought was eighteen, dressed in simple one-piece dresses that were torn and threadbare but clean. Nearly all girls he noted, with only two boys in evidence. The children were uniformly comely and the eldest, a girl, had a startling quality about her. Her face was pure oval, her eyes were a doe-like brown and her lips soft and tenderly expressive. Her body was of that softly rounded lightness which her dress, pulled in at the waist with a bit of faded ribbon, seemed to dignify rather than distract. Her hair was a soft black brown, long and free, pulled away from her face by another strip of ragged ribbon. She alone of the group seemed unabashed and she stepped down from the porch with the free grace of perfect health and a total lack of self-consciousness.

"Good morning, sir," she said to him over the split picket fence.

Colin snapped suddenly, too, and felt silly. "Good morning," he said a trifle hastily. "I—I didn't know anyone lived in these woods."

She smiled, her teeth gleaming in perfect rows. "Yes, sir. We've lived here a long time. I was born here.

Colin looked about him at the other children who began to come slowly from their hiding places. "And all these too?"

"Yes, sir … and my mother."

"What about your father?" and instantly he could have plucked out his tongue because he suddenly realized that this was the family Charley had told him of, omitting to tell him that they lived on his land.

The girl's feelings showed not so much by any movement of her features as by their cast iron lack of movement whatever. "He doesn't live here, sir."

Colin searched her face for any sign of coarseness, for any indication of inferiority of intellect, for stamps of temperamental imbalance but found nothing.

"I'm Mr. Taradon's head forester," said Colin in introduction. "Colin Campbell. I was searching through this area for some signs of pulp wood cutting. I haven't been able to locate any."

She pointed a slim arm toward the north and he noted a slight flush mounting her cheek as she spoke. "They were cutting about half a mile over there yesterday."

Colin eyed her closely. "Have they given you any trouble?"

The girl cast her eyes down at her feet. "Nn-n-no …"

"Look at me," he said in his curious cutting voice. He stepped close to her with only the gate between them. "Have they been giving you trouble?"

Her head came up and her chin tilted a little high. "You say you're the head forester?"

"Yes I am and if they've been bothering you I want to know it."

She breathed deeply and looked full into his eyes. "Mr. Prince and that bit yellow Negro of his make it impossible for my sister and I to even go to the spring. They caught her once."

Colin looked at the sixteen- or seventeen-year-old girl who stood shyly against the door facing of the house. Her body was a delight to the eye as was her sister's but lacked some of the exquisite details. Her breasts seemed about to burst the thin confinement of her shabby dress, her waist small and her legs strong and straight. Her face was comely but lacked the exquisite chiseling of the older girl.

Something sad, savage and irresistible took possession of Colin and his hands gripped the dry pickets till they cracked. He looked at the older girl, then at the younger one. "Come here," he ordered in a low hard voice. Slowly she came down the steps, her sharp nipples describing tiny circles on the thin fabric of her dress, making Colin's eyes blur out of focus.

"Yes, sir." She stood near her sister and looked at him with the trusting eyes of a spaniel.

Colin had trouble composing himself as the storm of rage that rose in his chest threatened to burst its bonds. "Did they hurt you?"

"No, sir."

This took Colin aback. "Even when you fought they didn't bang you about?"

"I didn't fight."

"You ..." He squeezed the gate pickets hard.

"No, sir. They were two big grown men and when they ran me out of breath and I saw I couldn't get away there was no use fighting. It would only have made matters worse."

The stripped-down logic of her remarks struck Colin a hard blow. What use, indeed, with two grown men who would have been thwarted only by some overpowering physical means which the girl did not have the strength to provide.

"She was sick for two days," supplied the elder sister. "Mother had to keep her sort of drunk on whiskey so she'd be quiet."

The iron hand gripping Colin by the throat seemed to tighten slowly. "Where is your mother?"

"Right here, sir." She stepped from behind the little set off kitchen wiping her floury hands on her apron. She was a striking woman, tall and strongly built and apparently none the worse for bearing a flock of children. Her face wore the look of calm resigned tragedy of the woman who had no friends and no associates other than her children and a man who visited her whenever the mood took him.

"I see my daughters are telling their troubles." She turned to the girls. "You shouldn't trouble the gentleman."

"On the contrary," he said quickly. "I practically forced it from them."

"I'm Irma," she said quietly. "The oldest daughter is Calla and this one is Rose. They're good girls, Mr. ..."

"Campbell."

"Yes, sir. They've always been good girls, but it is their misfortune to be beautiful. Luckily we live a long ways from people otherwise they might not be so good. Young blood runs strong, Mr. Campbell. They often go to the creek to swim … it's only half a mile down the hill and naturally they don't have bathing suits. I've been afraid this would happen ever since the cutters came so close, and I'm afraid it's our fault that they came. You see, Calla and Rose walked across the woods to where they were working. They don't have a lot of fun, sir, and I didn't try to keep them back. I think that's the reason cutting operations were moved so close to us."

"So that was it. I wondered and I was searching for them when I ran into your place. I didn't know you lived here."

"Yes, sir, we've lived here for twenty years. Mr. Taradon is a very kind man."

Colin thought of a million questions and dared ask none. What was Jim Stuerm doing housing his sub rosa family on Charley's land? Who supported them?

"Mr. Campbell, if you wouldn't mind eating in a colored person's house we'd be honored to have you. It'll be ready in a moment."

Crushing weights of anger, confusion and futility lifted momentarily from Colin's breast. He smiled broadly and bowed gallantly. "It is I who will be honored."

Rose giggled happily and Calla smiled her slow smile and opened the gate for him. "Mr. Campbell, will you have this rocker?" she offered as he came up on the porch. "It'll be cooler here."

"Thank you," said Colin, taking the chair. Rose sat at his feet on the steps and considered him through steady eyes, while Calla went into the kitchen to help her mother.

"You like living here, Rose?" asked Colin willing to do anything to relieve him of that embarrassing scrutiny.

Her round face dimpled delightfully as she smiled. "I guess so, sir. I've never been any other place."

"That's right, you haven't. How long ago did you have your … your trouble with those men?"

"That was a week ago, sir."

Colin let his eyes wander over her full luxurious figure unconsciously.

"It hasn't been time enough to tell yet," she said candidly.

Colin flushed scarlet and felt thirteen kinds of a fool. "Well … let's … er … hope not."

"Yes, sir. We don't think it will come to anything."

He was immeasurably relieved when dinner was announced. The older children sat at a small table with their mother and Colin while the others sat about with well piled plates in their laps.

Marney, the fifteen-year-old, just budding into round exciting womanhood sat on the edge of the kitchen table unconsciously exposing a long satiny leg complete from hip to ankle as her dress had become elevated by a splinter as she sat. Her face was quiet and her manners, if not perfect, were good and inoffensive as were the rest. During the meal there was no noisy demonstrations. They had cabbage, beets, field peas cooked with okra, corn bread, butter, and cool rich milk. Colin ate heartily, which made the mother beam with pleasure. Rose hardly took her eyes from Colin during the whole meal and he was acutely uncomfortable, glad of the occupation of eating which made it unnecessary to meet her frank gaze.

"Irma," said Colin curiously. "I find that all your children speak beautifully. They're well mannered and of course a great cut above the average in looks. Living back here like this and …" He stopped in confusion.

She smiled, "You mean … and being colored? Yes, sir, I suppose that does seem strange. However, it can be explained. You didn't say it but you must have noticed that I speak well, too. You see, I was a school teacher. I graduated from a teacher's college in Pennsylvania and struck out to help my benighted and down-trodden brethren. Naturally, when I arrived here I found that they weren't all that downtrodden and also that my idea that they were thirsting for knowledge and would leap at any opportunity to learn was wrong. Some of them did, of course, but the majority were content to farm and live. Maybe you haven't noticed it, Mr. Campbell, but a Negro has an infinite capacity for living."

He nodded. "I have noticed it and also that unhappiness isn't one of their long suits. They seem to be able to make the best of a situation."

"Yes, sir. Well, I met Mr. Stuerm and I stopped teaching school." She stopped and devoted her attention to her plate for a time. It seemed that she was silent more out of respect for Colin than herself. She raised candid brown eyes to his. "Education is impotent before love, Mr. Campbell. I found that out for myself. As for the children, I have done what I could to see that they were correctly brought up, though I have long since decided that I am not a good judge of what is or is not correct or right. I just did the best I knew how according to my lights."

"On that remark let me applaud," he replied earnestly. "You needn't censure yourself there. I've about decided that no one knows. One does what one can and that's the end of it. May I compliment you on your success with the children?"

"Thank you, sir. Mr. Taradon has been most helpful and generous."

He looked at her quickly then averted his eyes and started eating again.

"You were about to ask why Mr. Taradon instead of Mr. Stuerm?"

"Please, I didn't intend ..."

She smiled generously. "It's quite all right, Mr. Campbell. What pride I might have had along those lines has necessarily been subdued long ago. I accept Mr. Taradon's bounty because I have no choice in the matter. I cannot return his kindness because I have no means to do so. Mr. Stuerm was improvident. He couldn't provide decently for his legitimate family."

He felt a sad pity for this woman and her rock-like calm, the pointed objectivity of her words and her refusal to spare herself on a single point.

"I'm afraid we were squatters. Mr. Stuerm built this house for us as he was an excellent carpenter but he built it without Mr. Taradon's knowledge or consent. Mr. Stuerm died six months ago but he hadn't provided for us in a long long time."

Colin glanced at the shoddy clothing of the children. "Charley can do better than this."

"Please, sir, no!" Her face had gone white from the urgency in her voice. "He gives us what we ask for. Mr. Taradon is a man with a heart of gold and *we will not impose on him.*"

Colin eyed her steadily. "Irma, I thought you had done away with that sort of pride. You have three girls here who are becoming clothes conscious or will. It is unfair to them that they should have to wear old clothes. It isn't right. I can't give you any silence on this matter but I will promise you this. Anything over and above what Charley has been giving you will come from my pocket. I may tell him and I may not but I will say that whatever I bring here will not be from him but from me. You have become numb from all these years out here and I'm afraid maybe you now have a slightly distorted viewpoint which, of course, is forgivable and understandable. Thought must now be given to these children. They should have every advantage that can possibly be gotten for them, no matter how or where it comes from."

Irma's eyes dripped tears as she looked fixedly at her plate. "You're right, of course. I should have known you better. Big fierce men are very kind and very generous."

Colin flushed at the naked praise. "Never mind that." He rose to his feet. "I enjoyed the dinner, Irma. Thanks very much."

"Thank you, sir, and we all thank you for your interest, but please ..."

"That's all. Rose and Calla and the others shall have some things they can dress up in. They deserve it, Irma, and they're going to get it." To save himself further embarrassment he turned and walked out of the kitchen and leaped off the little porch which connected it to the house. Before he got to the gate he heard bare feet pounding after him. He turned and Calla stopped in sudden confusion.

"What is it, Calla?" His voice was soft and gentle so she took heart.

"Mr. Campbell," she began haltingly. "Are you really going to bring us some things?"

"Yes, I am," he said smiling. "Why?"

"Please, sir, would you get me some ... some silk ..." She flushed and lowered her eyes.

He laughed, "You mean some lingerie?"

"Yes, sir."

"Of course, and it won't be silk either because that wears out too fast; it'll be nylon."

Her eyes grew wide and her breath came quickly. "Thank you, sir ... and you don't have to get me anything else. Just some ... just that."

Colin's chest hurt in a queer exultant way as he caught her gently by the shoulders. "How you talk. Of course you'll get something else. Shoes, stockings and a dress or two."

"Just get the cloth, Mr. Campbell," said Marney as she approached, wide-eyed, on the tail end of the conversation. "Mother can make them a lot better than they do in stores."

"That's what I'll do, Marney, and what do you want especially?"

Marny looked away and twisted her shoulders in embarrassment, stealing glances at him. "Please, could I have a Mickey Mouse wrist watch? I don't really need any clothes because these are ..." She tried to cover up several unstrategic rents in her garment, "... it'll do for me."

Colin's eyes stung and his sight grew blurry. Suddenly he grabbed them both by the shoulders and hugged them hard. "You're damn right. You'll both get what you want and more besides." He wheeled quickly and walked to the jeep.

As he was about to get in Rose walked from some hiding place. He had not seen her approach. Her full lipped mouth wore a faintly provocative smile and again her gaze was direct and upsetting. Colin was hotly aware of her round smooth thighs sliding in sinuous rhythm beneath her thin skirt. His skin prickled and his nostrils pinched.

"You're going to where they're cutting, Mr. Campbell?"

"Well, that is ... yes, I am."

She slid into the seat beside him in a single fluid motion. "I'll go along to show you the way. You can drop me on the way back. I've never ridden in a car, you see." She twisted in her seat so she could watch him and Colin, without saying a word, touched the starter and drove away, sweating.

"What do you want in the way of clothes, Rose?" he asked not daring to look at her.

"Something red," she said succinctly.

"What about some underclothes."

"I don't know, sir. I never wore them and they're pretty, but I'd rather have a red dress."

"What about both?"

"Can I have both?"

"Certainly."

She clapped her hands ecstatically. "That'll be fine."

Colin collapsed over the wheel for a moment feeling that he had been through an ordeal by fire. This family was something that he had neither seen nor had any of his experiences prepared him for it.

"Mr. Campbell, what are you going to do to that yellow boy and Mr. Prince?"

Black anger flooded him anew and made his breath come with difficulty. "Plenty," he snapped shortly.

"I sure hope I get to see it," she replied with satisfaction. "I hate to be made to do anything."

He stole a glance at her on the strength of her last statement. Her knees pointed toward him as round as a melon and as he looked, the breeze blew her dress back, revealing two golden thighs of such alabaster smoothness that his stomach ached like a cramp. Though Rose had missed some of Calla's classic cut she had more than made up for it in sheer quality. She had a child's apparent total disregard for the effect her body had on others, yet Colin had the feeling that she wasn't entirely unaware of it.

At the top of a long hill she touched his arm and pointed. "Right down there, Mr. Campbell."

Colin sent the jeep plunging down the grade, deftly twisting it away from obstacles and between trees. Down near a little spring creek he found the pulp wood crew resting for lunch. The cutters were ahead of the loaders some two hundred yards, the nearest being two loaded trucks and their crews and a three mule team and a slide used to haul the cuts to the trucks from more inaccessible places. Colin skidded the jeep to a stop near the mules and got out.

The yellow Negro rose from his place at the base of a tree and approached, smiling a little. "What can I do for you, sir?"

His deference infuriated Colin. On the slide was a heavy whip with a short thick stock that the mule skinners had been using to touch up the animals when they balked. Colin picked it up and flicked it out to full length and considered it calmly. "Come over here."

The man lost his smile and after a moment's hesitation walked over within good reach. Colin pointed to the jeep. "See that girl there?" The man looked and his face grew muddy and splotched with dirty spots. He swallowed and words tumbled from his mouth. "She ain't nuthin' but a li'l ole nigger gal what …."

Crash! The whip had leaped out, exploded in the man's face with a report like a rifle. The man staggered and almost went to his knees, a bluish gash on his face. Again the whip licked out and cut a ragged wound in the forearm. A cry escaped the Negro's lips and he turned to flee but the lash wound around his ankle, throwing him heavily.

Suddenly Rose appeared at his elbow. "Please, sir, it wasn't him as much as it was the white man. He only caught me. He didn't do anything."

Breath whistled through Colin's nostrils as he stood over the man. "Get up," he grated and when the man hesitated stooped and lifted him bodily to his feet by his shirt front.

"If I ever even hear the slightest hint of you hanging around that house again by God I'll whip you within an inch of your life. She stopped me this time because it seems you were only a tool but from now on your presence within a mile of the house will be enough. Can you understand that?"

The other nodded, gasping with pain and fear. Colin released him and some of the fire died from his eyes. "Take him in," he said to the driver of a truck, "and let a doctor see him. Tell him to send me a bill in care of Fairview Plantation. Now, where's Prince?"

The wizened little Negro who had spoken to Colin before pointed his finger. "He comin' yonder," he said, scuttling close, speaking almost in a whisper. "He got a gun."

Colin went back to the jeep and took out his automatic and slid a cartridge into the chamber. Prince strode on with long widely spaced steps, walking with the sure balance of a trained man of the forest. When he neared the jeep, Colin raised his right hand, the automatic held steadily pointing toward the middle of Prince's stomach.

"You can stop there, John."

He stopped, eyeing Colin with calculated wariness.

"Turn around!"

Prince obeyed, holding both hands shoulder high. Colin tweaked the long barreled revolver from his waistband and threw it into the grass. A belt axe followed and a pocketknife came next.

"Okay, John, you can relax now for about ten seconds."

Colin handed the gun to Rose. "Get back in the car," he ordered sharply. He faced Prince again whose face had gone black with rage. "See that girl?"

"Yeah, I see the yellow whore, why?"

"I just wanted you to know when you wake up tomorrow or the next day why you look so much like a butchered beef, and I'll warn you before we begin that if I ever hear of you and that yellow Negro either separately or together being anywhere in the vicinity of that house again you'll regret it till the day you die."

As he finished his long left snapped out a hard nerve shattering slap on the cheek, sending Prince staggering backward. With a bellow of rage he lowered his head and charged in a bull-like rush to be straightened up and sent crashing to his back by a rocketing left uppercut that nearly tore his head off. Prince sat up and shook his head muzzily. He came to his feet more slowly this time, caution beginning to make its appeal to his consciousness.

Colin shuffled in and feinting him off balance with a left jab hooked a shattering right to his ribs. Again Prince caved in and stretched out on the grass. When finally he stood on his feet again his arms hung loosely and his eyes appeared glazed. Colin stepped in close and had the flashing realization of having made a mistake. A right swing came up and caught him flush on the point of the chin, sending him stumbling backward, falling flat on his back.

With a yell Prince leaped forward to work out on the fallen man with his feet but he had forgotten Rose. She leaped from the jeep with the pistol in her hand. She was afraid of it and didn't know how it worked but when she pulled the trigger and nothing happened she hurled it with all her strength into the man's face.

Colin staggered to his feet, his breath coming in stuttering gasps, his head ringing like a belfry. His sight was blurred and he saw two of everything. He shook his head finally clearing it enough to see Prince stretched at his feet.

"I had to stop him, Mr. Campbell," she sobbed, almost in hysterics. "I had to stop him. He was going to kick you to death while you were down."

Colin shook his head again and muttered, " 's all right, Rose … good job."

His head feeling clearer he bent over and inspected the fallen man. The pistol had struck him muzzle on, flush on the right cheek cutting a deep gash but doing no other damage. Colin hauled him to his feet and shook him hard. When he let him go Prince managed to stand. Colin waited till he had shaken most of the cobwebs from his brain then stepped in and, dodging a roundhouse right, clipped him a crisp one-two on the chin cutting him like a knife.

Neither blow had been calculated to put him away but to maim and injure. Prince staggered but didn't fall. Again he tried his head down charge that netted a clubbed hand rabbit punch on the back of the neck and almost drove him into the sod. Five minutes later he was a sobbing slobbering wreck, his spirit broken and his face a gory mess of pulped flesh and gristle.

Colin blew like a winded dragon and fastened his glance on the little colored man. "Bring me some water," and the little fellow leaped to obey.

"Got sumpn' else hyer whuts better," he confided after Colin had drunk and washed his hands, and slipped a pint bottle into the white man's pants pocket.

"Thanks," said Colin shortly. "What's your name?"

"Name Shawty Boles," he said in an undertone. "I ain't been able to fine out nuthin' yet."

"That's O.K., Shorty. Maybe later. You fellows had better get these two to the doctor. Mr. Prince isn't feeling too well, I'm afraid."

After seeing the truck leave with the two beaten men Colin wiped his wet hands on his sweat soaked trousers and climbed back in the jeep where Rose sat, her eyes shining with hero worship.

"Hot damn," she ejaculated as they moved off.

Colin smiled. "Did I do all right?"

She wriggled in her seat. "You sure did put the wood on them, didn't you? Gee, I wouldn't have missed that for a ... red dress."

As they bumped along toward the Stuerm house Rose pointed toward a cool green little valley. "The swimming hole is right down there. Why don't you drive by and take a swim?"

The idea had such manifold attractions that Colin without answering diverted the vehicle and soon they were parked on the edge of a bluff overlooking a round deep pool of cold spring water. Colin licked his lips with anticipation and before he was down the bluff to the water's edge he was nearly undressed. He felt the bottle in his pocket and taking it out took a deep drink. The fiery liquor nearly choked him but he managed to down it and even took another stiff one. He felt battered, sore and sticky but the drink had helped immeasurably. He sat in the sand by the water's edge and luxuriated in the feel of the hot abrasive on his naked buttocks. Reaching over he picked up the bottle and took another mighty pull chasing it with a handful of creek water.

His head now began a new and more delightful kind of buzz than that provided by Prince's roundhouse right which had so nearly ended the fight. He felt tall and immensely capable and leaping to his feet he dove cleanly into the water. He emerged gasping from the cold shock and blowing like a porpoise. Glancing up at the bluff he saw Rose standing there watching him with absorbed concentration.

He frowned. "Hey up there, do you usually stand around and watch men swim in the raw?"

She didn't answer but he could see the dimples in her cheeks deepen in a smile. Then before he could utter a word of protest or even move she reached down and catching the hem of her dress in her fingers stripped it over her head in one quick move- ment and Colin had the impression of being struck a hard blow with the most lasciviously constructed body in his experience. She took three quick bouncing steps to the edge of the bluff and soared out and down in a flashing dive, so perfect that her body entered the water with a soft plop, and the rebound splash was nothing to speak of.

She emerged from the water with a rush and flung her long black hair making a circle of drops around her. Her mouth was open in a broad smile of sheer animal exuberance and her eyes sparkled with good nature and fun. With a fast overhand crawl she swam to a log and almost leaped from the water to sit upon it, pushing her hair back behind her ears and stripping the water from her silken skin with her hands.

"Feels good, doesn't it?" she said breathing a little faster from exertion.

Colin had been frozen to such immobility that he went under and came up strangling and turkey red, her silvery laughter doing little to improve his state of mind. He simply could not avoid looking at her as she sat on the log her legs dangling in the water waving slowly to and fro like the fins of a fish.

"Is it a habit of yours," he said huskily, "to go swimming naked with strange men?"

Her teeth flashed in the sun. "No, sir. You're the first man I ever went swimming with."

He examined the opalescent sheen of her wet skin, the pout of her breasts like twin globes of golden fruit making triangles in her stomach where the sun was shaded away. She stretched, arching her back and again Colin groaned inwardly. He was in it now and there wasn't a thing he could do about it. Slowly and almost without conscious volition he swam toward her and finding that his feet could touch bottom he walked the last ten feet and stood before her in water a little more than waist depth.

"I guess you know you're a very naughty girl," he said.

She grinned at him. "Why?"

That had him—why indeed? It was an experience rare on his list and he'd be a fool if he denied it.

She absolutely had a magnetism that rocked him fore and aft. "Rose, go put your clothes on." It was a weak and spineless remark which impressed him as silly and her not at all.

She smiled and kicked the water with her feet. "Do you really want me to?"

He swallowed hard and opened his mouth to make a hard determined affirmative answer but to his dismay and utter surprise something entirely foreign came out instead. "You have the most totally upsetting body I think I ever saw. No wonder those men chased you."

She raised her arms above her head and bent backward slightly at the waist while blood thundered in Colin's head in a way that shook him terribly. Her eyes rested again on his face serious and melting.

"Stop it … stop it," he thought he wanted to say but he never did.

With a motion like a snake sliding over a branch she slid into the water. She was so near that her nipples touched him and their caress was pure pain. Colin wanted to back away and could not; he wanted to protest and couldn't utter a word. Her eyes were pools of deep mystery, soft and holding his with primitive attraction.

Then they were close and their arms were in the proper places and they were straining closer. Her breath, faster now, fanned Colin's neck and her body had a subtle pressure that was at the same time a movement. A strangled sound came from him as he bent and kissed her lush lips that parted for him, cool, fresh and as alive as though endowed with a life of their own. He stroked the length of her strong fine-skinned back and the water hardened bulges of her breasts bringing forth little gasps as though in half repressed agony. With a savage lunge he lifted her clear of the water and strode some twenty feet to the opposite shore that was smooth and grassy. He put her carefully down and followed, wincing as her sharp teeth bit the flesh near the crease of his armpit. His hands touched the underside of her thigh where the tendons stood out as hard as pencils.

"I can't stand it!" It was not a statement but a plea and her head went back into the grass with a convulsive jerk.

Some time later they lay quiescent but still close to each other, the violent winds of passion now quiet and nature satiated. Rose muzzled his shoulders with the cool nose of a puppy and her eyes smiled gratefully as he turned his head to look at her.

"What would you say if I told you you had been a bad girl?"

"Mr. Campbell, what is bad?" she asked with simple directness.

Colin's mind staggered to a halt trying to find something that didn't sound fatuous, trite, or stupid in answer to her question.

"Was what we did wrong?" she persisted.

Colin sighed. This was going to be harder than he had anticipated. "Some people seem to think so, Rose. Besides that, it's dangerous."

Rose's sniff disposed of the danger. "And I don't see how anything so wonderful can be bad."

Again Colin was thrown for a loop. She turned her spaniel soft eyes on him. "Didn't you think it was wonderful, Mr. Campbell?"

That was one thing he could answer with complete honesty. "Yes, Rose, it was wonderful."

She smiled with a satisfied air. "Then it's all right. You think so and I think so. There isn't anyone else concerned."

She twisted sideways to get the lowering sun from her eyes which threw her breasts into full silhouetted prominence, making Colin squirm inwardly. She had such a totally unaffected air about her, such honest, forward, breath-taking seductiveness that he fought to provide himself with an adequate description. She turned to face him and drawing her heels beneath her sat on them, her knees close together. He wanted to look away but the sculptured triangle of her stomach and thighs drew his gaze from the grasp of his will with the ease of a toothpick drawn from a mound of ice cream. His muscles quivered and brought him to his knees within inches of hers. There he stopped knowing that she would provide his conscience with the necessary balm by closing the gap. With a fluttering sigh she did so and the touch of her smooth belly and the points of her breasts turned his arms into convulsive clutching bands.

Colin crawled shakily into the jeep and Rose got in on the other side. "Mr. Campbell, don't be worried about me. If I get pregnant it'll be that other man."

He frowned. "How can you be so positive about that?"

She smiled and slid down in the seat relaxed and comfortable. "Mother has a book."

"And you've read it?"

"Yes, sir. We've all read it—those over thirteen. She makes us read it and we talk about anything we don't understand."

"Apparently your mother didn't read it herself," commented Colin dryly.

Rose laughed. "That's what Calla told her. Mother likes children, Mr. Campbell. She doesn't regret a single one of us. She said so."

He sighed as he slowed down for the little house nestled in the heart of the clump of great trees.

He stopped the jeep and Rose turned to him. Impulsively she touched his hand at the wheel.

"You won't worry, Mr. Campbell?"

He swallowed hard. "No, Rose, I won't worry."

"And you'll come back?"

He eyed her hard, a heavy hurt in his chest and his mind a brawl with truth and conscience having a battle royal. "Rose, I wish you weren't so young. I can't honestly tell you ..."

She slipped from the jeep her face tranquil and a half smile touching her face. "You don't have to tell me anything,

Mr. Campbell. Maybe I'm young but, you know, sometimes I seem to know things that I shouldn't know—that no one ever taught me. When I jumped in the water it was because I wanted you and I knew I'd get you. You'll be back, sir. I go to the creek every day about this time in the afternoon and about ten-thirty in the morning. Good night, Mr. Campbell."

She turned and sprang away in a lithe bounding run.

Colin wiped the sweat that had suddenly beaded his brow. He worked the shift into first.

CHAPTER EIGHT

THERE WAS A party in progress at the residence of the John Sanford Beldings and from the local notables present things other than bridge were likely to be discussed. Sheriff Denny Potter, Ben Miller and his son, Sturges, Jackson Roberts, and a certain Fred Renshaw whose position was not apparent as he did not share in the Miller, Roberts, Belding enterprises, nor was he a local politician. The party had been progressing for some time and Sturges Miller had taken on a notable load of beverage, dodged in sequence the lardy blandishments of Belding's two hundred pound daughter, her ninety-eight pound six foot cousin and Lucy Roberts, who had what it took but was such a complete fool that she was hazardous entertainment.

Sturges ducked behind a superfluous potted palm in the over-sized lounge which passed for the "ball room" in Belding's amazing palace of plaster cupids, bad lithographs, pseudo Ionic columns and pseudo Gothic turrets. Sturges hated this house with its shrieking confusion and tasteless rococo pretentiousness. As he stood there, grateful for the respite, dragging deeply on a cigarette, he saw a man and a woman pass on their way to the terrace which flanked the western side of the house. French doors let out on this flagged area which was confined by a wall with potted plants scattered about with abandon but little taste. Sturges piqued by curiosity peered out from his hiding place. His face grew hard and taut with little white compression dimples showing about his lips, as turning away he walked out into the ball room.

A heavy hand fell on his shoulder and Sturges turned around. "Come, my boy," boomed John Belding. "We're to have a little conversation which I'm sure might interest you." Belding was short, fat, balding, and acutely conscious of it. His face resembled a bit of very disappointed pastry fashioned by some young housewife whose introduction to cooking had been recent and disastrous.

Sturges shrugged the hand from his shoulder with distaste. "I doubt it," he said shortly, "but it should have something by way of entertainment or nuisance value."

Belding, whose voice strove to be as big as his body was round, bellowed with laughter. "Always the wit, always the wit. Boy, you should have gone on the stage!"

"Many a true word in jest is spoken. Lead on, John, and I follow with misgivings and a faint hope that I can at least get some laughs from this caucus."

Belding laughed again and led the way into the library where brandy had been poured and cigars lighted. Roberts, a thin nervous little man with gimlet eyes, rolled oats' complexion and wisps of hair of no particular color scattered over his tight-skinned pate like some ancient, motheaten skin rug, sat tense and stiff on the arm of a chair whose covering had been stuffed to bursting, so much so that it scarcely resembled a sitting accommodation. Ben Miller sat sprawled out in another chair, the twin of that occupied by Roberts. Ben was as gross as an elephant and not a lot smaller. Temper, too much rich food and whiskey had made his face a relief map etched over with purple capillaries and acne scars. His teeth were still hard and firm with a curious resemblance to mossy head stones in an old cemetery.

"Sit down, Sturges," said Ben Miller, "and watch politics at work. Y' gotta learn sometime."

Sturges looked stonily at his father. "Why?" The question fell brick hard and curiously flat, stopping conversation. Everyone was now staring at Sturges.

Belding shook with mirth. "I told him a while ago he oughta be on the stage. Boy's got a sense of humor."

The others smiled but Ben glowered at his son who sat back in a deep chair and appeared to be thinking of going to sleep.

"Where's Renshaw," asked Roberts, his voice dry and raspy like the song of a locust.

There was some headshaking and Sturges sat up in his chair. "The last time I saw him he was telling Mercedes the story of his life on the terrace. Just why the story of his life should entail such enthusiastic use of Mercedes I can't imagine."

"What do you mean?" asked his father, frowning heavily.

The boy shrugged. "Well, to begin with they were standing quite close together. From where I stood it appeared that he was giving her a Swedish massage."

Faces grew embarrassed and turned away but Miller growled, "Don't be crude, Sturge."

Sturges laughed loudly and collapsed into his chair. "Very well, father. I retract my statement."

"They were discussing Tibetan architecture at a distance of ten feet."

"I'm sure Mr. Renshaw was conducting himself like a gentleman," said the father heavily.

"Well, I wouldn't know anything about that. Where would he acquire such esoteric habits?"

Belding's laugh was somewhat more forced than the others had been but at this point Renshaw walked into the room.

"Been waiting for you, Fred," boomed Belding.

Fred Renshaw looked little like the popular conception of a politician. He was tall, rangy and had a certain powerful calm about him which was accented by his soft drawl. His face was strong and craggy with a broad forehead and crisply curling iron gray hair. He would have a strong appeal to certain types of women.

"Well, I'm here. What's the beef tonight?"

"We got elections coming up," said Ben Miller, "and we got a few private nuts to crack."

Renshaw poured himself a stiff hooker of brandy and sat down. "Pulp wood botherin' you, huh?"

Sturges sat straighter and began to examine the man. He cared nothing for his twenty-five-year-old stepmother and didn't particularly hold it against the man if he chose to slip in a little necking. Ben had picked Mercedes up in a New Orleans French Quarter club where she was headlined as, "The Girl with the Million Dollar Torso." This bit of press agentry was not too florid because she did have a lush body but in the brain department she had a sense of opportunity and a two-handed acquisitiveness which stood her very well in lieu of the usual cranial content.

"How did you know about the pulp wood deal," growled Belding, lighting a fresh cigar.

Renshaw smiled. "I know everything about everybody. I even know about the secret safe at Ben's camp but none of you ever told me about it. Was that nice, boys?"

Sudden awful silence settled for twenty seconds and again Belding was forced to call on his heavy laughter to ease the stiffness.

"I'll tell you boys something," said Renshaw, lighting a cigarette. "This is one time where you're going to have to play it on top of the table."

Ben Miller reared up in his chair. "What'd 'ye mean by that?"

"I mean I can't have any rough stuff going on around here at this time. I've played ball with you, Ben, and the rest of you because it suited me. I've let you climb the ladder and pass for the wheel horses hereabouts but I'm afraid the picking's going to start leaning off from now on."

A chorus of incredulous queries leaped at him from all sides. He held up his hands and smiled. "Come, now, fellows, everyone's had a good time so why bellow. All of you are well fixed …"

"But I want to know what's come over you," roared Ben Miller, his face turning purple.

Renshaw shrugged. "The times, my boy, the times. It seems that you pulled a few that you had no intention of me knowing anything about. That wasn't a very friendly attitude. For instance, just how did you manage to get that pulp wood contract from old man Taradon? And what's this thing that's building up here about the time it is due to expire? Who, exactly is this long, lean, white-headed gent who has moved in with Taradon? I've heard some disquieting rumors and since none of you have made any effort to discover anything about him I've made a few discrete inquiries and I find that he's from Washington."

All previous silences were noisy compared to the one which dropped on the room nor could Belding find any excuse for letting go a leveling burst of mirth. Miller had turned gray and Roberts appeared about to burst into tears.

Renshaw stood up. "So, I'm afraid I'll have to cast you boys adrift. Maybe you don't know it but Taradon and Whit Wallace are bosom buddies and what do you think you can do to keep him out of the Governor's Mansion come November? It so happens that there are times when no machine or a combination of machines can beat a certain personality. Generally they find it convenient to go along and if you'll recall this present machine was built by Wallace several years back. If we don't go along with him we'll find ourselves sitting on the ground with the wreck in neat piles about our ears."

Sturges began to sober rapidly. So the trio weren't as potent as they had appeared. Renshaw, whoever and whatever he was, seemed to be the wheel while the others just rode along.

"Now," continued Renshaw, his voice taking on a tougher tone as he stood up, "I'm going to tell you something in two-syllable, easily understandable words. Just advice, mind you, because as of now you and I are just acquaintances. You have been a money grabbing pack of dunces. You have stooped to some things that makes my stomach roll over. You're considering more such moves right now ..." He glanced at Potter who was looking deflated. "In spite of Potter's verdicts of accidental death, I don't like them and I'm having no truck with guys who play that way. I'm a politician. Maybe I sometimes play rough and close to the margin but I'm not a gangster nor do I condone the methods. My advice is to take the best deal you can get from Taradon. Get rid of Potter because if you don't, just having him available might make you play it too fast and loose."

"I don't get rid of that easy, Mr. Renshaw," said Potter who had recovered some of his ginger.

The man looked at Potter coolly. "I'm certain you don't and I'm not really concerned—just giving advice. Now, just who this Scotsman Campbell is or what his official connection with the government is I can't say. My informant couldn't find out so you can just let your imagination run a little if you want to. I wouldn't advise using any of your clumsy frames on him, though. He might get irritated and if he did then Washington might become concerned which I'm sure you wouldn't like. Now, take you, Roberts. I'm sure all the bottled stuff you get from Louisiana is strictly on the up and up but what about that tank truck of yours that has been painted so many times; that has probably discovered more routes to Kentucky than the highway maps show. It would surprise me no end if it turned out that that 'Butane' had been taxed."

Sturges was as near sobriety as was humanly possible for anyone who had taken on such a quantity of alcohol. He was thoroughly interested. Roberts on the other hand looked as though he had suddenly been stricken with acute appendicitis. He slid over into his chair; he had been perching tensely on the arm and licked his dry lips. Miller and Belding were speechless and still in their chairs.

Potter alone seemed to have recovered. He smiled, "What do you know of me, Mr. Renshaw?"

Renshaw lit a cigarette with maddening deliberation. "Not a whole lot, Denny, but I could start with that girl you put to bed with Jack Taradon. Of course, it might turn out that she was already dead when you or your stooges put those fingermarks on her throat but it'd be rough if it didn't, wouldn't it?"

It was now Potter's turn to sink back in his chair pale and quiet.

It took all this time for Ben Miller to find his voice and when he did it shook the room. "A goddam yellow-bellied quitter. A stinkin' son of a bitching rat ... Well, let me tell you something, Mr. Wise Guy Renshaw, if we can't work with you we'll work without you and just remember we got other methods we can use too, so keep your good advice to yourself."

Renshaw started to his feet but the sharp voice of Sturges stopped him.

"Other methods?" said the boy, his voice ringing against the rococo walls. "You mean like taking flash photos of people in intimate moments?"

Again that catastrophic silence during which no one seemed to breathe.

Miller got slowly to his feet. "You're drunk—get out."

Sturges bowed deeply. "It'll be a pleasure, a distinct pleasure." He turned on his heel and left the room.

Renshaw looked at Miller through eyes that were calm but burning. "That, too," he said softly. "My cross will be the fact that I was ever seen with people like you."

"Then shoulder your cross and get moving," said Belding coming to his feet and lending his heavy voice in support.

"There's just one thing more, gentlemen," said Renshaw softly as he wound a snowy handkerchief tightly around his right hand. "Miller, I never liked you but your stupidity and money were helpful. However, our association included nothing that will make me accept what you called me. That's my one weakness. You're a dog and what you said was nothing but your bark, but I didn't like it."

He swung a terrific right that moved so swiftly and caught them all so by surprise that before they could even speak Miller was stretched full length on the floor, his eyes glazed and set.

Renshaw took three long steps and stood in the door, "I bid you good evening, gentlemen."

"You let him get away," snarled Miller five minutes later.

Potter to whom the complaint had been delivered demurred, "Like a rattlesnake. He can go fast and far for all of me. Didn't you hear what he said? That guy's got a knife in us and if he knows, then there must be plenty more that knows."

"That is absolutely right," squealed Roberts becoming vocal. "How *do* you suppose he got all that information, and by the way, Miller, what does Sturges know about that picture?"

Miller shook his head muzzily. "I ain't got any idea. Wasn't nobody supposed to know about that but Timms who took it and us four ... now, goddamit there's been a leak and I aim to find out where it is."

Belding sighed and poured himself a stiff drink. "That's fine talk but you know good and well ain't a one of us told nobody."

"Well, if we didn't, then who did?" bellowed Miller, purpling.

"What about Timms?" asked Roberts trying to still his trembling lips with a finger.

"Timms was killed at Kassarine Pass, you fool," snarled Miller. "He left here a week after he took that picture. Sturges was in the Pacific with the Marines, Timms was in the Army and they didn't have a chance to get together."

"Well," Roberts sat down so hard he bounced, "*someone* has been talking and not only about the picture. If you'll remember, Renshaw didn't seem to know about that so the thing is complicated more than ever."

"What I want to know," said Potter, "is what'll we do now?"

Miller reared back in the chair. "Just like I said, we'll do without. We got the county and a finger in plenty more. We got a sheriff and a judge. If Renshaw thinks that just 'cause he's out we'll suck in our bellies and quit he's got another think comin'. Who's with me?"

"You know me," said Belding heartily.

"I'm stickin'," said Potter. "But things are gonna have to change a little. We can't stand no investigation and we don't want Washington in here."

"This is bad," moaned Roberts, wringing his hands. "We don't know where we stand. How much of what Renshaw knows can be proved? I'm too old to go to jail."

"Ain't nobody goin' to jail," roared Miller, gnawing his cigar fiercely. "And you're in whether you like it or not, Roberts. I ain't never thought much of your guts and be damned if I want you runnin' loose with what *you* know. You'll stay in and like it."

As Renshaw opened his car door Sturges spoke to him, stepping from the shadow of a lagustrum. "How much of what you said can be proved, Mr. Renshaw?"

The man grinned engagingly. "Nothing, son. I know so little that my talk sometimes scares me. I happened to be on the beam tonight on all points which are nothing to me but rumors. A smarter bunch of men would have just laughed at me. You saw the result tonight."

"There's going to be trouble here," said Sturges dully.

"There'd better not be," said Renshaw crisply. "That much was the truth of what I advised them. Since the war, son, everybody had been investigating everybody else and you see what a stink it caused. They started on John Kellaway, the aircraft man, and John being no fool turned the light on three or four senators and got out from under like an eel and left the senators battling it out, dashing hither and yon trying to get the investigations stopped. One even wrote another and told him that if he didn't lay off he'd have *him* investigated and so on. The taxpayer has begun to get self-conscious. He realizes now that he's footing the bills and he's getting mad. Maybe it's a cycle and maybe it's permanent, but I'm hoping it's permanent. I'm a professional politician but no one could ever say I deliberately rooked a taxpayer unless you consider getting fools elected comes in that category. I'm having no hand in any final burst of pyrotechnic glory that your dad and his buddies are riding for. I could stick and probably profit but even I have certain limits and principles, believe it or not."

"Somehow I do believe you," said Sturges strangely moved. "I didn't think there were any more left."

Renshaw smiled. "Some, I'm glad to say. I don't know what they're grooming you for, son, but whatever it is I'd hand it back to them because when they fall they're going to pull the whole structure down with them and everyone around at the time'll get burned."

"I've been thinking about that. Thanks a lot, Mr. Renshaw. I'll remember you." They shook hands and parted.

An hour later a loud pounding sounded on Sturges' door. He slipped on a robe and opened the door. His father clumped in and sat solidly in an insufficient, straight chair. His eyes burned feverishly as he looked at his son. "Now, suppose you tell me what the hell was the matter with you tonight?"

Sturges put his hands into the pockets of his robe and stared back. "In what particular way?"

"Makin' them remarks about your mother …"

"Stepmother," corrected the other sharply.

"Awright, stepmother … and your attitude and remark about that picture. What do you know about a picture?"

"Nothing, except that there is one and who it is of. I don't know what you intend to do with it."

"How'd you find out?"

"I'm not at liberty to reveal that."

"Timms tell you?"

"Who's he?"

"That tramp photographer who worked a couple of months for Roberts at the paper."

"Never heard of him. What do you intend to do with the picture?"

Miller's eyes narrowed. "Suppose you tell me whose side you're on before I make any such announcements."

It had come and now Sturges was faced with the decision. He took a deep breath and faced his father squarely. "In view of what Renshaw said tonight and the looks on the faces of all of you, it would appear that I'm living in a nest of gangsters and double dealing the like of which I've read about but never thought really happened. Personally, if I were you I'd take the man's advice but since you won't then you can count me out."

Miller was silent for a while. "Desertin' your own flesh and blood on the word of a ward heeler, a two bit crook of a politician—is that it?"

"I didn't choose my flesh and blood. Mother died pretty early and now I don't wonder. She wasn't very smart but she wasn't a gun moll. She got out the only way she could. I'm taking a better way because I can."

"You do," Miller's voice was hard and the blood in his face was heavy and dark, "and you'll pack and get now. Of course, you won't expect to be remembered in the will, either."

Sturges stood silently for a moment, then turned and went to a closet and pulling out several gladstone bags began to pack.

"I'm tellin' you," bellowed the father. "If you go you'll be cut off without a cent."

"You said that once. If you don't mind, I'm busy."

Miller stood up and with a look of extreme bafflement, turned and left the room.

Frantic barking by Charley Taradon's big setter woke Colin from a deep sleep. He donned a pair of khaki pants and picked up his pistol from the bedside table. He worked a cartridge into the chamber and walked out on the verandah. "Who's there?"

"It's me, Sturges. Call off your dog."

Colin spoke to the setter who obeyed and slunk back to the edge of the verandah.

"O.K., you can come in now."

Sturges stepped from his coupe and strode up the brick walk. "Think you could put a guy up for the night?"

"Certainly. What's the trouble?" asked Colin.

"Want to talk about it now or wait till morning? I have some news."

"Tell me now and take a chair over there."

Sturges sat and related the events of the night. "So, now I'm on the grass."

"And you feel that they intend to use the picture?"

"Yes, I do. When Renshaw told them that he knew their other tactics Dad came up with this other method or methods. That's when I came in about the picture. I thought they'd have heart failure. When Dad came in to give me my walking papers he wanted to know where I had found out about the picture and when I told him I couldn't tell him he told me I'd better decide what side I was on and I did. Think Charley can use an extra man?"

"Yes. Jesse's tower is being taken care of by two men who split it between them and that leaves other towers empty half the time. Think you could become a forester?"

"I could try. Of course, I wouldn't want to make it my life's work but I'll stick 'til this thing comes to a head."

"That's fair enough. Let's hit the hay. We'll see Charley in the morning."

Charley was amenable and right after breakfast Sturges was taken out into the woods in the jeep by Willie.

"You," said Colin accusingly to Charley, "didn't tell me you knew the next governor."

"This might sound like a lie, boy, but I didn't even know he was runnin'. Told me the last time he was here that he might but I don't read no more and I wouldn't listen to a campaign speech on the radio fer no money. Things is gonna be different if he gits in. That there man is like Huey Long. He kin beat any machine then he makes his own. I'll say this fer'm though. He ain't never misused his power 'less you'd call gittin' a lot of sorry men 'lected on his ticket but I guess he can't help that always."

Colin lit a cigarette and pondered for a moment. "In one way the news that Sturges brings is welcome, in another way it isn't."

"How's that?"

"Well, I got a story from Willie. Dug it from him by main strength you might say ... I hate to tell you this, Charley, but I'm practically forced to."

"Hell ... go ahead," trumpeted the old man.

"Where's Donna?"

"I saw her on King a few minutes before we came out here. What's she got to do with it?"

"Charley, this is going to take a lot of understanding from you and maybe it's going to be hard because it's something to do with the fine points of human psychology which you might not be too well versed in."

"Git on with it. Psychology ain't nuthin' but a six bit word fer horse sense."

"A few days before Jack went into the Army he came home drunk one night and insisted that Donna help him into the house. Willie took her the word so she came out and together they helped him into his room. He had been gotten to in some way and the whole thing was a set up because Willie states on his oath that Jack wasn't anything like as drunk that night as he had been at other times past. Still he insisted that Donna come out to help him in. After they had gone to Jack's room and Willie had been sent to get some milk for him he tore the robe from her and threw her on the bed. He was somewhat drunk, it is certain, because he had forgotten about Willie who came back at the worst time, of course. Willie took to his heels but as he was leaving the house he saw a brilliant white light flash. He asked me about that and the only thing I could think of was a flash bulb and I also knew what such a picture could mean to the Combine. I told Sturges to try to find out if they had such a picture and last night he very cleverly did so. They have it and if they can't use politics on you, which is to say coercion, then they will fall back on that picture."

Charley spat his quid into the yard and lowered himself slowly into his chair where he seemed to deflate like a punctured bladder. His face grew old and his eyes seemed to recede in his head. When he spoke his voice was a hoarse whisper. "Goddam son of a bitch. 'Twarn't nuthin' in God's creation he wouldn't do … nuthin'."

"I'm sorry I had to tell you this because I knew it'd be a shock, but the way things are shaping up I thought you ought to know."

"How would they use it?" whispered the old man, his eyes burning feverishly.

"I don't think they ever considered using it because they feel certain that if they threatened you with it you'd give in."

"Yeah, but s'posen I didn't, how would they use it? Wouldn't publish nuthin' like that, would they?"

"They wouldn't have to. They could have a slew of prints made and … well, say they gave John Prince a dozen and told him to distribute them around among his cronies who would probably love to have something like that to put in their billfolds. Then they'd manage to let a bunch of teen-age boys have some … such distribution as that. Naturally it wouldn't ever get to that."

Charley shook his white head. "What a thing to happen! She'd be ruint … ruint fer life."

Colin looked quizzically at the old man. "Then you don't think she's ruined already—from the incident, I mean?"

"Nope. She was a young 'un—sorta wild and wooly. She was nuts about Jack. 'Twarn't no rape more'n likely. Son, you can't expect too much of folks—never could. There's a lot of sons o' bitches like Jack but who knows how much of that was my fault? Donna's a fine gal. I don't care what she done when she was fifteen but wasn't that Jack the devil's elbow? A goddamn low down bastard. To top his own kin and have somebody outside to take a pitchure of it. Wonder how they managed to git him to agree to that?"

"Maybe the same sort of pressure they put on you?"

Charley nodded. "Could be." He reached up and pulled himself from his chair with difficulty. "Think I'll go lay down for a while. I don't feel so good."

Colin let him go, feeling sick and bruised at the old man's grief. He sat longer gripping the arms of his chair. Why did people do the things they did? Take the incident with Rose. Why had he taken the fruit of her offerings? Why didn't he feel repentant? Where was the usual remorse and feeling of disgust and hatred? If, he reasoned, a man can't actually stop himself at such times then it's a pretty good thing that he didn't feel remorse or he'd ruin his health and mental outlook as well.

Colin worked on his jeep till dinner. He was relieved to see that Charley had come out of his low mood somewhat and made a mental note that the old man still had a lot of steel left in him. He had also revealed an unsuspected knowledge of humanity. Charley was no fool in spite of his lack of formal education.

Donna was unusually quiet and left immediately the meal was over. When in certain moods she loved to get on her horse and ride and of late she was riding a great deal.

Seated on the verandah after the meal Colin said, "I'd sure like to get a look in that safe Sturges told me about."

Charley spat lustily from his perch on the shelf. "Whut you think they got in it?"

"I'd say about half a million dollars in black market proceeds and untaxed income, incriminating papers, and the picture and negative most likely."

"Thinking about doin' a little safe crackin'?"

"I'd do it in a minute if I knew how to go about it. I mentioned it to Sturges when we got up this morning but he reminded me that they keep anywhere from three to five men there at all times."

Charley gazed out across the broad front pasture and massaged his tough leathery jaw. "Twouldn't do to be seen in that neck of the woods. Let 'em git jes' one thing agin us and they'll paint it on every housetop in the county. That'd be right down their alley."

"That's what'd make it difficult. There must be a way though. I'll give it some thought."

A ragged little boy came around the side of the house with a small flour sack on his shoulder. "Good morning, Mr. Taradon—Mr. Campbell." His voice was softly modulated, respectful but unafraid.

"B'goddam if it ain't Jimmy. Come on in and set, son. Colin, this here is Jimmy Steurm."

"I think I saw Jimmy yesterday. I found the house, Charley."

"Y'did? Well …" Charley seemed embarrassed. "What you bring me, son?"

"Mother sent you two quarts of watermelon rind preserves. She said you like them a lot."

"A fact, a fact. You take 'em back in the kitchen to Lilla. Tell her I say to give you a bag of that candy …no, better take all you can carry or your sisters and brothers won't git none."

Charley turned pink. "Keep candy here fer the kids … sometimes kids come around and …" He stopped and mopped his perspiring face.

Colin felt a suspicious tightness in his throat. "You big loud-mouth tough acting sissy. I ate dinner with the Stuerms yesterday and I got the whole story. Stuerm must have been something of a character … building that house on your land and not saying anything …"

Charley wriggled with embarrassment. "I done whut I could. Jim wasn't no good and ..." He let the sentence trickle away to nothing.

"I want to buy some things for them. Those girls are beautiful. They are well behaved and I don't know when I've been attracted to a family like I was to them."

Charley grinned. "I been teasin' George Hall 'bout them gals. Looks like it's you."

Colin laughed. "I'm afraid George would be prejudiced except at night. I'm not a bit. Where I come from there aren't enough Negroes to be anything like a problem so I never grew up with any resentment."

"Me neither," said Charley spitting accurately. "It was a hell of a lot of it all 'round me but I never latched onto none. I don't resent no livin' man ner beast 'cept when they step on me and the color ain't whut riles me. Them's a fine bunch o' kids even if I do jerry George 'bout 'em sometimes."

"It might interest you to know then that John Prince with the help of that big yellow Negro raped one of them not long ago."

The old man turned so white that Colin cursed himself for mentioning it.

"They done what ... Who to ..." He leaned forward tensely.

"Rose. They outran her and seeing that she was overpowered she sensibly gave up so she didn't get hurt. It'll be some day before they try it again. I cut that Negro to pieces with a whip until Rose stopped me by telling me that he had only helped Prince. Then Prince came up and I tried to kill him."

Charley sat back in his chair and sighed. "What the hell is the world comin' to."

"Rose seemed very philosophical about it, though. It made her sick for a couple of days but she got over it all right."

"I was 'fraid it was Calla. That gal is made of fine stuff, fine drawn I mean, like a race horse or a blooded heifer. Rose is a rugged gal and can take such things a lot better. I'm glad you worked Prince over. I guess he'll begin to wonder if it ain't a pretty bad thing to work on my land."

"If he ever goes near that house again," said Colin passionately, "I'll have need for your governor friend and everyone else I can find."

"Kinda hot on that subject ain't you, son?"

"Yes and there's only a line between a couple of touchy subjects. Now listen to this and maybe you'll think I'm as bad as Prince."

Colin told him everything that transpired at the creek almost detail for detail as well as the dialogue that went on between he and Rose.

Charley grinned so widely that he showed his back teeth. "Damned if you ain't the beatenes' man ever I seen in my life. What sort of a fellow is you anyhow?"

Colin lit a cigarette with an angry flourish. "I'm me, Charley, and every now and then I ask myself if that's good or bad?"

"That depends on a lot of things. If you set yourself to be a tin Jesus then it would be bad but you don't do that. You do what you want to then you come back here and confess it all to me in spite of the fact that you're just about to fall in love with Donna."

It was Colin's turn to redden and he did so. "So I'm a dog. If that's so then I just can't help it. I tried to kid myself but it's no use. After that kid dove into the water with me I was a gone goslin' and she knew it. She has something very much like second sight or clairvoyance."

"You listen to me, boy. There was one o' them poet fellows once named Burns and he writ somethin' about a man bein' a man fer a' that. Men ain't changed none since they started walkin' on two legs. Give me a honest son of a bitch any day to a mealy-mouth, dark time operator."

Colin felt a quick rush of affection for the old man. "Thanks, Charley. That helps a lot."

Charley shrugged. "I ain't got no eddication to howl about but I kin add two and two. What you gonna take them kids?"

"I thought I'd buy some clothes for the oldest girls but the more I think about it the more I see that I can't do that. I'll have to get something for the others, too. Think of it, Charley, Marny said that her old clothes would do if she could have a Mickey Mouse wrist watch."

Charley turned his face away and looked out across the pasture. He was silent for a while, thinking. "I'll bet them kids wear out every Sears Roebuck catalog they find just lookin'."

Colin sighed. "Yes, I suppose so. One has the impulse to take them out of their environment and give them a chance for the so-called better things, but the older I get the more I wonder what these *better* things really are. As they are they are happy, unspoiled, natural and all out in the open. The world would teach them lying, cheating, all sorts of deceit, treachery and the love of the almighty dollar. I just don't know."

Charley shook his head. "Me neither. I can't even find the heart to cuss Jim Stuerm fer bein' a loose livin' damned fool. If it takes his kind to help bring kids like them into the world you kin almost fergive him fer bein' what he was. Git 'em whatever you want and charge it to me."

"No," said Colin positively. "You've done your part. This is on me."

CHAPTER NINE

WHEN BEN MILLER and Semple arrived the next morning neither Charley nor Colin was surprised. Ben was bluff and hearty and carried a copy of the contract that was due to expire soon. "Thought you'd want to get this thing in on time, Charley," he said waving the contract. "That way I won't lose no cuttin' and you won't lose no money. Sorry about that log cuttin' deal. I'm makin' Prince pay for 'em out of his wages."

"Mr. Semple didn't tell you what our terms are then," said Colin, hoping to smoke the matter out into the open.

Semple nodded vigorously. "I told him but Ben thought he and Charley could come to terms."

"Then," said Charley with a snort, "Ben ain't a bit smarter'n he was ten years ago. You got a contract made out, Colin?"

"Yes, I have."

"Git it then. Ben, you kin tear up that there piece of paper fer all the good it'll do you."

Miller's eyes narrowed nastily. "I'd like to get this thing done all friendly-like Charley, but your memory ain't that short that you can't remember that I wasn't as dumb ten years ago as you try to make out."

Charley took a big chew of Brown's Mule and swung himself to his perch and masticated rapidly. "Time'll tell who was dumb when," he said easily. Colin came out of the house and handed Miller the contract he had drawn up.

"There it is," he said. "That's the way it'll go this time." Miller began reading and the further he read the blacker his brow became. Finally he snapped it back to Colin. "You don't think I'd sign no such robber notice as that, do you?"

Colin shrugged but Charley answered him. "Ain't nobody astin' you to sign nuthin'. Go git your pulp wood sommers else and see who gives a damn."

Miller placed his hands carefully on his fat knees. "It ain't that simple and you know it. Think I like doin' business with you? It's buy wood from you or go out of business and I ain't goin' out of business and you can bank on it."

"I'm listenin'," said Charley.

Miller breathed deeply and looked at Semple who looked at everyone besides looking scared. "Well, you don't leave me no choice." He dug into his inside coat pocket and pulled forth a five by seven glossy print and extended it toward Charley. Like a cat Colin pounced on it and tore it away from him. He took a quick glance, enough to assure himself that it was a perfect shot, then paling so that his eyes were a shocking contrast to the rest of his face, tore the picture to bits and put them in his pocket.

"I see you know about the picture," said Miller with a harsh chuckle. "Tearing it up didn't do no good. There's plenty where that come from."

"So your idee is just some more blackmail, eh, Ben?"

"Call it what you want to, Charley. I aim to have my pulp wood and I don't want no monkey business."

Charley spat into the yard and his deep-set eyes burned with the steady fires of a strong man's hate. "What's your terms?"

Both Miller and Semple relaxed and smiled. Miller flourished the paper. "Why, just the same contract as before, with a few changes."

"That's what I thought," said Charley, pulling a tobacco stem from his mouth. "Well, you kin come back on the date the contract expires and we'll talk business."

"What's the matter with now?"

"I'm takin' all the time I got," said the other with a snarl. "I ain't in no hurry to do business with a dog."

Miller's smile was not nice. "I'm too horny hided to bother about your back talk, Charley. I'll be back," he flourished the paper, "and you'll sign ... just like you did before."

As Semple and Miller walked toward their car the old man dropped into his chair and breathed heavily. "We got to do somethin', son."

Colin nodded and scratched his head. "I'm going to have to take a look at that camp. The safe is the only answer."

Sturges found it fun to sit in George's tower and examine the landscape through a pair of powerful binoculars. He could see quail playing in open spaces and in the late afternoon rabbits came out to dash about in play, chasing each other or sitting sedately munching tender grass. When he did his stint at Jesse's tower he began to search the surrounding country as was his habit. Early one morning when he had climbed to the tower and seated himself comfortably he began a minute inspection of the area covered by the tower. The creek wound deviously through the woods to a spot about half a mile away then curved east and south. Directly in the curve he had discovered a rather large round pool and resolved to take a swim in it when he got a chance. Today he re-examined the spot with care, then gave voice to a smothered exclamation.

Three women, young girls they seemed, stepped from the bushes completely nude. One was just beginning to bud into what would be a wonderful body. One was on the full blown side, not too much so but enough that he could see her bountiful charms with ease. The third was a model of classic line. Her long beautifully rounded legs moved with the subtle grace of a dancer and her waist was small and trim.

Sturges shifted his attention higher and gasped. Beads of sweat began to form on his forehead as he feverishly sought to focus the glasses to a finer degree. For an hour he watched them as they plunged and swam about or dived with the grace of waterfowl from the high bank of the stream. When they left he reported to tower five that he was leaving his tower to do some investigation and climbed rapidly down to the ground. At a breakneck run he cut through the woods trying to intercept them coming closer he noticed to a big grove of seeder pines. So headlong was his stride that when he burst out into a little clearing and saw them looking at him curiously he almost fell so suddenly did he stop.

"Hi," he said feeling very silly.

"Good evening," said the one who had seemed the oldest and most beautiful of the trio.

Sturges searched mentally for a good dark hole in which to take a dive. He was embarrassed before these three pairs of frankly questioning eyes.

"I ... I ... thought I saw ..."

Rose said, "Was that why you were running?"

Sturges flushed deeply. "Not exact ... not, I, you see ..."

With a sudden rush of feeling for this white man who was manifestly embarrassed to a considerable degree, Calla stepped into the breach. "My name is Calla, sir. This is Rose and the other one is Marny. They're my sisters."

Sturges could have kissed her for any number of reasons. "Well," he said with a deep breath. "I'm glad to know you."

"I think you should know, sir," said Calla looking him straight in the eye, "we're Negroes."

The shock was such that he reeled both figuratively and bodily, the look of contempt thrown at him with such unaffected candor being of the reverse of help and as they passed from sight through the brush he leaned against a small tree and strove to collect himself.

After a time he walked over to the little spring that bubbled deep in the green lined recesses of an ancient barrel and sat down. Hazily he considered the barrel, noting that the bands had rusted and left only dim red streaks to show where they had been attesting to the identity of the container. The overflow ran gurgling down a hill on its way to the creek.

Calla stepped lightly through the last fringe of brush carrying a bucket and stood facing him.

"I'm sorry if I offended you a while ago," he said frankly.

She searched his face for an uncomfortable interlude. "Yes, sir."

He grinned engagingly, so much so that she smiled a little in return. "That doesn't mean a lot," he said chidingly. "You haven't said that I'm forgiven."

"Forgiven for what, sir?"

Sturges fielded the pitch clumsily. "Well ... I mean ... I guess I must have offended you in some way. I'm really sorry." A great deal more of his heart went into that avowal than he had intended.

The girl must have noticed it because she smiled. "I guess it was a little shocking to find that we're colored?"

"You're a smart girl, Calla. You can see where I might have been shocked but can't you see that I'm sorry I let it show?"

"I'd much rather know," she pointed out with crystal logic.

"That isn't what I mean," he said a little angry at his poor efforts.

"What do you mean, sir?"

He took a deep breath and came to a momentous decision. He stood and walked over till he faced her at close range. "Calla, I'm a white man, reared in all the petty superstitions and prejudices common to the race. I am considered well educated but I know that my education has not removed the impressions of a lifetime spent in this part of the country. When you told me that you were colored I was shocked first because I hadn't considered it as even possible. Second, because it occurred to me that life had handed you a rotten deal. I'm not sorry I did it because that was part of me reacting. I am sorry if it offended you or suggested in any way that you are some sort of lesser person. Please believe me."

Sturges met her calm searching gaze with deadly resolution. He would not falter no matter how much his spirit cried out to take those searching eyes from their portals. The girl's sensitive face twitched faintly about the mouth and again her slow smile turned on the light.

"Thank you, sir," she said in a soft melodious voice. "I don't think anyone ever talked like that to me before."

Sturges would have spoken if he could have thought of anything to say. As it was he stood there and watched her as she dipped the battered old bucket in the clear cold water, her arms showing up strong, round and tinted delightfully in gold and ivory. As she knelt and bent over her short skirt came up showing six inches of thigh of such ineffable smoothness that his skin prickled. He heard himself speaking and sounding far away like another person.

"I'm Sturges Miller. I'm working for Mr. Taradon as a forester."

She rose from the spring, her bucket spilling out water from being too full. She faced him again and said, "Yes, sir."

He was nonplussed. He didn't want her to leave but he could think of nothing to say that might keep her there.

Once again she came to his rescue. She put the bucket down and sat gracefully on the grass drawing her legs under her Turkish fashion. "Do you like it here?"

He sighed gratefully and sat near her. "Woods used to be just a place to get wood or go hunting. Since I've been out here I feel entirely different about them."

She looked off into the distance. "I've never been ten miles from here. I don't know anything else but I love it, too. We have books and from what I've read the outside world frightens me."

"It should. The outside world has very little to recommend it if you're not accustomed to it. Its hold on people is mostly habit, the things they've become accustomed to."

Calla rose to her feet. "I guess I ought to be going now. Mother will want the water."

Sturges rose also. "There isn't any good way that I can tell you what meeting you has meant to me," he said with frank simplicity. "I'm glad I met you and I want to meet you again."

She smiled a little wider this time. "Yes, sir. I'm kind of glad I met you, too. I'd like to see you again but won't people talk … I mean if they know you've been talking … I mean talking to me … like this, sort of …?"

He shrugged with vast indifference. "I suppose they would, but right now I can't seem to be bothered about anything except when and where I'll see you again."

"You could come to the house."

Sturges frowned and realized that if he didn't brush this away quickly she might get offended again. "Would your mother approve?"

"I don't know, sir. I could ask her."

He sighed heavily. "I'm afraid the world would be against us. She probably wouldn't approve of a white man coming to see you."

The girl's smooth forehead furrowed. "I don't know. A colored boy wanted to come to see me once and she wouldn't allow that."

"Ask her, Calla, and meet me here at this time tomorrow ... will you?"

"Yes, sir ... I'll ask her. And Mr. Miller ..."

"Yes?"

"Why do you want to come to see me?"

It took Sturges several seconds to recover from this devastating broadside. In a single flash a million things burned through his mind with blinding speed but at the helm was that one powerful thought that stayed with him. Anything but complete, utter honesty to this unspoiled child would be a sacrilege. He said, "Because, Calla, you are the most beautiful girl I have ever seen in my life."

Her face remained impassive but he could see a little pulse beating at the base of her throat and a slight tremor seemed to go over her. Her voice was as soft as the note of a cello. "Thank you, Mr. Miller ... thank you very much." She turned and was gone.

It was eight o'clock next morning when Sturges saw Colin's jeep come bouncing down the narrow dirt road toward his cabin. With almost a sob of relief he dashed out of the door catching the toe of his shoe on the sill and falling heavily in the dusty yard. He got up and brushed himself off, grinning as Colin's lusty bellow of laughter reached him.

"That form off a diving board could get you a place on the Olympic team," yelled Colin.

"Shut up and get out. I was just anxious to flag you before you passed by."

"Why all that anxious?"

The other's face grew serious. "I have to talk to someone."

Colin clambered from his vehicle. "Not wanting out already, are you?"

"Oh, hell no. I like it out here. Something else entirely."

"We'll take up your troubles later. I want some info on your Dad's camp."

"Like what?"

"Like what sort of road leads there from the highway. How close to it the woods grow ... everything."

The other thought a while. "I haven't been there for a good while but as I remember it there is a narrow country road, about two miles in length, from the highway. It has gravel on it and can be traveled in all sorts of weather. The woods hover right over it. There is a yard of sorts but in town you wouldn't say it was on a lot any bigger than one hundred by two hundred. Everything else is woods, except the front of course which opens right on the river. Why?"

Colin propped himself against the jeep and lit a cigarette. "Your dad was out yesterday morning and handed us the ultimatum. Either we sign his contract or he spreads the picture. Frankly, I don't think he actually wants to do it. He's just using it as a threat, but as long as he has it the threat is there."

Sturges spat with distaste. "Boy, that's getting down real low. I wish I'd have had sense enough not to get drunk the other night. I might have been better able to find out things."

"You've already found out more than I ever thought you would. How many men does he keep around the place?"

"That I couldn't tell you. What are you thinking of, cracking the safe?"

"Yes. I don't see anything left to do. We've *got* to get that negative and pictures."

"How do you figure to do it?"

Colin frowned and spat a bit of tobacco from his nether lip. "You have me there. I've got to know more about it."

"Sorry I can't help more. Whatever you do you can count on me."

"Thanks. Now, what was it you wanted to talk about?"

Sturges walked around the car and got in. "Come on and sit down. I can't talk standing up."

They sat and Sturges thought hard for a moment. "Colin, I rammed my head into a situation yesterday that threw me like I never expected to get thrown. I wasn't ready for it, I had no defenses, and I still don't more than half believe it happened."

Colin waited, saying nothing.

The other was silent for a few minutes. "What would you say if I told you that I was falling in love with a Negro girl?"

In that instant Colin knew what had happened, but he carefully kept his face expressionless. "I could say a number of things, among which would be that you must have done a sight of adjusting considering how and where you were reared."

"I didn't do any adjusting," said Sturges doggedly. "In fact, I don't seem to have anything to do with it, period. It just happened and if I had been under ether the outcome couldn't have been any less of my doing. I can't explain it—it just happened."

Colin nodded, thinking of some things that had *happened* to him with which he had had little to do. "It has happened before. I take it that you have seen Calla."

"That's right and, brother, I don't even know my name any more. I'm just a cooked goose. What do you think I ought to do?"

"That's not for me to say. What do *you* think you ought to do?"

"I've stopped trying to think. All I can think of is her calm beauty, her flawless skin and the wonder of her body. I tell you she's out of this world."

"You realize," said Colin carefully extinguishing his cigarette, "that the attraction is just physical ... so far, I mean."

"No, I don't realize that," said the other stubbornly. "Her sister Rose has a much more exciting body. There's something ... call it silly if you want to, but there's something that just sort of reached out and sucked me in. I seemed totally without any volition or will. If she should turn into a female Svengali I'd not turn a hair. Does that sound silly to you?"

"It might if I hadn't seen her and hadn't had an experience with Rose. Of course, their poverty accentuates all of it. They manage to seem sort of regal in spite of their poor station."

"Of course," said Sturges excitedly, "that dress she had on wasn't ragged or torn. It was of the purest material. On her sack cloth would be a robe of divinity."

Colin laughed, and clapped Sturges on the back. "Boy you've got it all right. You've got a beautiful girl and a problem I wouldn't have for all the chopsticks in China. How far has it progressed?"

"I'm to meet her today to see if her mother will let me come to the house to see her."

Colin stroked his jaw. "One'll get you ten you win."

"What makes you say that?"

"I don't know exactly. Something about the mother, I guess. If the kid falls in love with you that'll sway mom. I gathered ... on my own of course that to her love is everything and justifies every sacrifice. Still ..."

"What?"

"I was about to say that if Calla does fall in love with you then your own responsibility is tripled. I think the custom is to keep her in a little house in the background like they live in, marry a white girl to keep in the big house and raise a herd of kids in both places. Somehow I don't have you pegged like that."

Sturges' strong teeth ground together. "You think anything would be bothering me if I had any such ideas? Hell, I'd have everything all planned out. As it is I'm in a funk, brother. A dark blue one."

"There aren't but two answers," said Colin gently, "and you know it. You have two alternatives. Of course, one of these alternatives might take any number of forms but broadly speaking that's all you have."

"What are they?" said the other dully.

"Take her North or to some other place where you can feel certain no one will ever see you that might tell off on you. Leave in such a way that no one will suspect that you're taking her. Let her follow later, that would be better. Marry her and cut this part of your life completely out. The other is to follow local precedent."

"The thought of marrying a Negro doesn't feaze you at all, does it?"

Colin shrugged. "You people all have the silliest idea about such things. Calla's father was a white man. That takes care of half. I rather suspect that her mother is no more than one eighth or one quarter Negro. With that tiny dribble of dark blood to you she is still a Negro ... I don't get it."

"I don't either," he said dejectedly. "I'm just pointing out what others will say."

"Sure, you have little enough choice there, I know. I've decided that even a good rumor would be enough to ruin a person down here."

Sturges sat straight again. "Well, God only knows what'll come of it. If I had the guts I'd run but I guess I'm just a weak sister."

"You could have avoided that lie," said Colin warmly. "It'll take a lot more guts to stick it out than it would to duck out and you know it. It'll take some scheming, too."

Sturges held his head in his hands. "Even now, talking to you about it, it seems unreal. It couldn't have happened but it did. I can't be in love with her but every molecule of my brain tells me I am. I saw her once … yesterday. It's today and I'm unnerved, and in pain. I don't even know how she'll feel towards me … the whole thing is screwy."

"Every man who was ever in love," Colin reminded him, "has felt that in some way his own particular case was different. And who can, in truth, say that it wasn't."

"With people being what they are, I'd say it is pretty likely."

"Right! Well, I have to be shoving. I've got to make all the towers today. I hope you can work this out right, Sturges, but I want to say one thing. Don't play loose with that kid."

"You need have no fear on that score," said Sturges strongly. "If I ever hurt her it'll be because I can't help myself and I'll get it worse than she." He stepped from the vehicle and Colin started the motor and pulled away down the hill to the creek.

Colin came to the top of the long hill from which he could see the grove of seeder trees and stopped the jeep under a gum tree. Its foliage was heavy and afforded him cool shade. He stepped from the car and sat, supporting his back against the rough bole of the tree. For a long time he looked across the little valley to the tall trees as they stood in silent majesty, wondering all the while, like Sturges, what it was about the family which held such a strong attraction. Was it their calm acceptance of life which had not in the usual sense been kind to them? Was it pity for the fine healthy children who had been born with a man-made stigma? He chewed up a grass stem and considered a visit. At the thought a queer little knot grew in the region of his solar plexus, and when Rose stepped from the brush not twenty feet away it became almost a pain but he was not surprised.

She stopped and smiled slowly, provocatively. "Good morning, Mr. Campbell."

He frowned severely. "How the devil did you know I was here?"

Dimples grew deep in her cheeks. "I heard your car a long way off."

"And you knew I'd be right here?"

"Yes, sir. I thought you'd stop here to decide whether you'd come to see me or not."

He gazed at her with something akin to fear. "You knew all that?"

She walked over with her languid graceful stride and sat beside him. "Yes, sir. I told you you'd come back."

Colin sighed and looked away. Just the presence of her, the knowledge that she sat near him made his blood race madly and this angered him. Her insufficient dress had slipped up a little as she sat and again the sight of her incredibly smooth thighs started the same hammering in his head.

"I thought you said you'd wait near the swimming hole," he said.

She shrugged lightly. "I thought about that and I decided that on account of the kids maybe it wasn't such a good place."

"You didn't seem to think so the other day."

She picked up a stick and began to make figures on the ground. "I don't suppose I did much thinking the other day."

He was silent for a while and she looked up at him leaning closer. "Are you mad at me, Mr. Campbell?"

The pain in his chest bit him again. He patted her hand. "Of course not, Rose. You just upset me. There's something about you that ... oh, hell, I don't know. I do know that your seeing me is no good." He breathed heavily. It was an effort to talk to Rose because of her absolute lack of worldliness and upsetting bluntness. "Suppose you'd fall in love with me, Rose?"

"Yes, sir?"

"Well, dammit you'd be hurt. I'm in love with someone else and when I marry I won't be able to see you any more and that would hurt you."

She thought that over a while. "Yes," she sighed, "I guess if you didn't come back I'd be disappointed. I'm willing to take the chance, Mr. Campbell, no matter what happens."

"But, Rose, I don't want to make you unhappy."

"I'm happy whenever you come."

"I know, but what if I stayed away?"

"I did all right before you came."

"But now that I have come, wouldn't it make a difference if I stayed away?"

"Yes, sir. I wouldn't have you any more."

Colin halted, baffled. She had now uncoiled and was leaning toward him on one hand with her legs parallel and bent at the knees. The neck of her poor dress was stretched taut by the bounty which it covered but could not conceal, revealing the deep cleft and the smooth rise of her breasts on either side.

"Rose, suppose I saw you several times a week all summer, then let's say I'd get married in the fall and stop seeing you, how would you feel?"

"I'd miss you," she said simply looking directly into his eyes.

"Wouldn't you hate me for treating you that way?"

She sat up suddenly her eyes flooding with tears. "Oh, no, Mr. Campbell, I couldn't *ever* hate you, no matter what you did."

Colin pulled at the lobe of his ear, the truth of her statement striking him like the flat of an axe. She really couldn't hate anyone. It wasn't in her. If he were a man …

She seemed to divine the trend of his thoughts, and placing a soft hand on his arm she crept close. "Mr. Campbell, can't we ... you and I just ... I mean can't we enjoy us and not think about the future? I won't ever bother you ... ever. If you come I'll be glad but if you can't come I'll understand. Maybe I sound silly sort of and young but you see I am young and maybe I can't talk as well as Mother or Calla but I know what I feel. I just want you to know that I'll be here whenever you come and when you can come I'll be glad. Can't we have it that ..."

She stopped because his hard arms were around her and the slight beard on his chin was scratching her face with a delightful abrasive pain. She clung to him and welded herself to every outline of his body returning his kiss hungrily.

He drew back finally, winded. "Damn you, Rose, I could wring your neck."

She smiled dimpling and laid her head against his chest, her soft black hair tickling his nose. Her dress had become disheveled exposing almost the entire length of her left leg and Colin, caressing it, savored the electric shock of her fine skin, drawing little gasps from her. She raised her head.

"Right down there," she said pointing, "there's a little spring branch. I found a little tiny hole about a mile away. It has a little sand bar on one side and it's almost covered with trees and vines."

He lifted her to her feet and held her close for a moment, then they climbed in the jeep and rolled down the hill. The little pool was like something out of a fairy tale. Hardly twenty feet across it looked cold and deep and on one side was a little beach some eight feet wide and ten feet long. Trees and vines had woven an impenetrable roof overhead making it a perfect hideout. Colin spread an army blanket on the sand and once more drew her close. Her mouth was avid and the movements of her body almost drove him mad. He reached down and catching the hem of her dress drew it over her head. She stood straight and unashamed, the beauty of her young body almost a physical pain to him. She fell against him hard, her breath whistling through her clenched teeth and his arms went around her, drawing her warm pulsating body close.

CHAPTER TEN

I F SHORTY BOLES had turned down that last shot of gin the night before and had been a little easier for his immense wife to rout from bed, John Prince would have probably told Red Norwood to go to the office for the new saws. As it was Shorty arrived fifteen minutes late panting and anxious to do anything which might turn attention away from the fact that he had been late. If Red had done the errand instead of Shorty many things might have been different. When the little man arrived at the outer office and was on the point of entering Ben Miller lumbered up.

"What you want, nigger?" he said thickly, having washed his toast down with liberal amounts of Bradsher's Special Age.

Shorty mangled the tattered hat in his hands. "Mistuh Prince, he say t' tell Mistuh Jeffery us got to have three new saws. Us broke one and de uthers ..."

"Okay," said Miller as he stumbled through the door.

The windows were open and Shorty's ears were preternaturally sharp, missing no word of a conversation that ensued between Miller and Belding. He picked his teeth with a sliver of wood and squinted disinterestedly at nothing but kept his ear bent toward the window. He absorbed and filed away all he heard.

By the time Sturges heard the sound of footfalls coming through the brush toward the spring he had trodden down a considerable area of grass and his face was damp with perspiration although the day was not particularly hot. Calla stepped gracefully into the clearing pushing a blackberry vine carefully aside with her fingertips. Her hair had been brushed back and confined at the nape of her neck with a scarlet ribbon and her faded dress was spotlessly clean and ironed. She smiled bewitchingly.

"Good afternoon, Mr. Miller."

"What'd she say," he burst out. He stopped and passed a trembling hand over his face. "I'm sorry, Calla. Good afternoon." He had corrected his urgency but he was still of the same frame of mind. She walked over to the spring and unhooking an old gourd dipper from the side of the barrel dipped up some water and drank. She smiled at him again and sat down, her eyes shyly inviting him to join her.

He walked over and flopped down beside her. "Did you ask your mother?"

"Yes, sir, I asked her."

"Well, what did she say?"

"She asked me if I loved you."

Sturges swayed, feeling like he had had a terrific drink of straight whiskey. "What did you say?"

"I said I had only met you yesterday." She stopped and her deep brown eyes considered him for a moment.

He felt that she had said more so he asked her. She nodded.

"Yes, sir, I told her that I hadn't talked much with you, and as far as I knew you just wanted to see me. Mr. Miller, white men want to see colored girls for just one thing, don't they?"

Sturges almost groaned aloud. "As much as I hate to admit it, Calla, I'm afraid you're correct."

"Is that why you wanted to see me?" There was that creeping suggestion of hurt contempt which he had seen in her eyes the day before. Couldn't she be a little less blunt?

He shook his head. "*No!* This is one time you're wrong. I told you yesterday that I wanted to see you because you are the most beautiful woman I have ever seen. That still stands."

He must have sounded hurt or desperate … he was desperate that she understand him … because she touched his hand very gently as it lay beside her on the grass and said, "Thank you Mr. Miller. I believe you."

He was so relieved that he had an insane desire to laugh … wildly. "What did your mother say about you seeing me?"

"She wants to talk to you."

He gulped painfully. "When?"

"Any time you can come."

He massaged his hair distractedly. "Do you want me to talk to her?"

Her eyes were serious. "I'm afraid I don't understand. You were the one who wanted to see her."

"Er … yes, of course. I'll see her. I just wanted to know how you felt about it."

"If she'll allow it I'd like to see you Mr. Miller. I've never been around men much. White men … never."

"Did your mother think it odd that a white man wanted to come to see you?"

Her smile was as bright as sunlight. "No sir. You see, my father was a white man."

Sturges took a firm grip on himself and stood up. "I'm going to see her now," he said almost truculently. With a single fluid motion she also stood up. He was foolishly aware that he had missed a chance to touch her by helping her up. Without a word she started toward the house.

Calla opened the yard gate for him and Sturges walked like an automaton up the brick path, his eyes on the tall striking woman who stood calmly near the steps. He could see the children all about; they had stopped playing when he came up and were looking at him curiously. His face felt hot and his stomach fairly writhed with tension.

"I'm Sturges Miller," he croaked scarcely recognizing his own voice.

The woman smiled. "Good afternoon, sir, I'm Calla's mother, Irma. Won't you sit down?"

He sat, feeling that if he had not he would have fallen.

Irma turned to Calla. "You and the children go to the back of the house and stay there till I call you." Her voice was modulated and kind.

Calla herded the children from the front of the yard to the back and Sturges didn't hear a single protest. His face grew unbearably hot as he fought for some opening that did not sound as ridiculous as he felt.

"Mr. Miller, you need not be uncomfortable. There is much about what you have on your mind that I understand perfectly. Believe me it is not my intention to cause you any embarrassment or to hurt your feelings in any way. I merely have a mother's concern for the welfare of her daughter."

Unaccountably he suddenly felt very close to tears and the musical soothing quality of her voice had a magical effect, making him feel a great deal better. He had, he now saw, an intelligent person to deal with and the discovery cheered him almost as much as had Irma's kindly voice.

He grinned boyishly. "You are a very understanding person, not to mention perceptive. I was in a kind of pickle because believe me a boy facing his first day in school is infinitely better prepared for what is ahead of him than I am. I don't mind admitting that since I saw Calla yesterday I have fairly wallowed in confusion."

"I can understand that, sir. Such situations occur very seldom."

"You have no idea how seldom. I ... I guess we had to meet, Irma, but now that we have met I don't know what to say ... how to start ... I'm over my depth and have been since I saw her."

Irma smiled knowingly. "You think my daughter is very beautiful, don't you, Mr. Miller?"

"I do with all my heart. So beautiful that if I hadn't seen her ..."

"And the sight upset you as it would any man."

"It did. I won't deny it, but if you are looking at me saying 'Here is another white man who wants a pretty colored girl' I believe you'd be doing me an injustice."

"I wasn't about to say that, Mr. Miller. I would have found out though."

Sturges mopped his perspiring brow with his handkerchief. "Yes, you would ... I'd bet on it."

"I believe you wanted my permission to see Calla?"

"Yes ... I do."

"Surely you realize, Mr. Miller, that you could see Calla without my permission?"

He nodded heavily. "I may have had such a realization subconsciously but I'm glad to say it never entered my head to act on it."

"I believe you, Mr. Miller. I think you are a very honorable man."

He flushed. "I didn't think so myself, haven't been lately, I mean. I guess maybe I was just weak."

She smiled. "I think you mean you have found yourself recently."

Sturges was so numb that the wonder of how she knew this didn't penetrate. "Will you allow me to see Calla, Irma?" He had to get it over with.

"Oh, yes, sir. As often as you like."

He gulped his throat dry and raspy. "You will, just like that ... no questions?"

"A few, sir, but I feel fairly sure of the answers. First, do you love Calla, Mr. Miller?"

He drew a shuddering breath. "You will find this hard to believe, maybe unbelievable entirely. I've seen Calla twice and during that time I have possibly spoken two hundred words to her, less probably. I'm sitting here listening to myself talk in a disembodied way. It isn't even me talking. Since I met her I've been drawn around by the nose. I have no will, no volition. The very thought of the fact sounds utterly impossible yet as I know that night follows day I know I love her."

They were both silent for a long time and feeling the silence he looked up. Irma's eyes were wet with tears. "It is not often that you can see a man walk out of himself and stand bare before you. The psychology of the human rarely allows it. I've seen you that way, Mr. Miller, and I'm glad. It speaks volumes for you and shows that you haven't hidden anything. You couldn't ... not now, not talking about Calla."

He hung his head and said huskily, "That's right, not about Calla."

"What will you do, sir? Calla is young but she is very intelligent, precociously so. She is not unaware of her beauty. You are young also and I dare say your blood runs swiftly and warm. If you come to see her, what will happen?"

He gripped his hands together till his knuckles cracked. "I know what you mean. I told myself yesterday that if I followed this down someone stood an excellent chance of getting terribly hurt. I can't sit here and in honesty tell you that I *know* what'll happen. I know what I want to happen and what I'll bend every effort in my power to see happen but I refuse to make a statement which we both know might or might not be true."

"I've said, sir, that you are a very honorable man. I was never more sure of it than now. On the other hand we are all human. I'm grateful for your honesty and I feel very sure that you'll make every effort to protect her in whatever way the term can be used in this case. I find myself with a family of fine children that I don't know what to do with. I can't expect them to live and die here under these pines never having a chance to live full lives of their own but I do hate to see them unhappy. In a way, Mr. Miller, I'm really glad that you came along. You'll be the beginning but not the end. You and Calla will be the experiment from which I may be able to guide the others."

"Calla said you wouldn't allow the colored boys to come here."

Irma nodded firmly. "I don't, sir. If that sounds snobbish or narrow I'm sorry. It is true that in the eyes of people we are Negroes. It is a genetic fact that I am only one-sixth Negro; they are much less because their father was a white man. If there is any difference whatever in the races then we are white not black, from a preponderance of white blood. Some of my family are quite black and I honor them none the less for it but with the blood that my children have it is not fair to thrust them back where privileges are fewer, where prejudice can reach them, where they will be shunted aside and made to struggle for their bare existence."

"What else can you do, Irma?"

She smiled softly. "Love, Mr. Miller, has made you do something unheard of in this country. I'm hoping that your love for Calla, someone else's love for the others can do something. Maybe it can't, maybe they will end up being some man's mistress just like their mother but times are changing and I want them to ride the crest and not drown in the backwash."

"That," said Sturges, his eyes blank with a kind of admiring wonder, "is strong philosophy. It has backbone and a goal.

I came seeking one thing and will leave with that and something else."

"And on your side," she said simply, "you have given me hope and you have showed me at least a way to begin something which I did not know how to start. It may be that I shall ask you for help."

"And I shall be glad to do anything in my power to see that your philosophy bears fruit because I see what you are trying to achieve."

Irma stood up. "I haven't felt this light and free for years, Mr. Miller. Will you accept the thanks of a mother who did not know what to do, which way to turn?"

He stood, also. "I will and you honor me. None of us are out of the woods. We are just starting but thanks to you I now can see my direction. I know now what lies ahead and it doesn't frighten me any more. Unseen things are the ones which seem to pose the greatest danger."

Irma wiped two warm tears from her eyes and walked to the end of the little porch. "Tell the children that they may do as they please now, Calla."

Calla came around the corner of the house her eyes bright and wide with question. She looked at her mother then at Sturges who grinned and winked at her.

"Come up here, Calla," said her mother gently. "Mr. Miller has asked that he be allowed to come to see you. I have given my permission."

The girl stepped forward and kissed her mother's cheek. "Thank you, Mother." No pyrotechnics, no wild enthusiasm, just the simple gratitude of a girl whose mother had granted a request.

Sturges touched her on the shoulder. "I'll have to be going now, Calla. I've got to go back to the tower and report and take a look."

She turned and said, "I'll go as far as the spring with you. We'll be needing some water."

Side by side they walked through the grove and into the underbrush which screened the spring from the house. "You have a wonderful mother, Calla."

"Yes, very wonderful. She must have liked you."

"I'm glad to say I think she did. When can I see you?"

"Any time you wish, Mr. Miller."

They stopped in the little clearing by the spring and for a moment the silence was stiff and embarrassing to the man. The girl seemed incapable of the emotion.

He faced her and stepping close said, "Every time I look at you you're more beautiful than the time before. How do you do it?"

She smiled, showing her perfect teeth. "I don't know, sir. I'm glad you think so."

He reached up and caught her shoulders. It was their first touch and it did things to both of them. Sturges felt the warm soft flesh with the wonder of a man who thought of it a great deal and found it just as he had expected. The girl's eyes grew serious and widened a little, her breasts reacted to her increased respiration. He drew her closer to him, hearing as from far away the thud of the bucket as she unconsciously let it slip from her fingers. Her eyes held his, steadily projecting a certain delightful wonder that was being born in them. She did not resist nor did she fall into his arms but allowed him to draw her closer, till he could feel with a distinct physical shock, her breasts touching him, their soft firmness sending rapturous charges through his nervous system.

He did not immediately kiss her. He held her close still looking into her eyes, feeling the firmness of her strong back muscles like the thews of some graceful animal. He passed a wondering hand over one side of her face smoothing back stray tendrils of hair and tasting the satin smoothness of her cheek through the sensitive skin of his fingers.

Suddenly he bent over and found her half open mouth, soft, moist and tender. The delicious pain of exultation flashed through him and he held her tighter, his lips hungry and drinking unutterable delights like nectar from the upturned cup of her mouth. Suddenly she broke away and sank to the ground her head bowed forward, sobs shaking her shoulders. He dropped beside her.

"Calla ... Calla ... what is the matter? Was I too rough ... did I hurt you? Please tell me ... I'm sorry."

She raised her tear-streaked face, her lips quivering and trying to smile. "You ... you ... didn't hurt me. I mean it ... you ..." She held her face in her hands and cried softly for a minute during which time Sturges writhed in pain. What had he done to make her cry? She looked at him again and this time the smile managed to make itself a little deeper. "I'm sorry I'm such a baby," she said, "but all of a sudden ..." She stopped and caught him by the shoulders and laid her head against his breast and cried again. Her sobs gradually slackened and then stopped. "I can't understand why I did it," she complained, an occasional sob shaking her. "It just went all over me and my knees got weak and I had to cry."

He held her close like a child and stroked her soft hair.

She looked up timidly. "I've never been kissed before—by a man. I guess I didn't know what it would be like."

"I didn't either," said the other meaning every word of it. "It never happened like that before." He let her go back, his arm under her shoulders till she touched the ground and he kissed her again. Her lips were as soft as petals, and their youthful inexperienced sweetness reacting like a drug. He could feel the hard outline of her teeth and the shattering touch of her hesitant tongue on the tip of his questing one.

He sat up wondering what actually happened within the body of a man that he could stand such terrific emotion and still function. He turned his head and looked down on the lithe delightful slimness of her body, its classic sculpture and pureness lines. Her eyes had the soft sated smoothness of a woman who is very sure of her control of the man she loves. He grinned and sank to one elbow, his face close over hers.

"You may be young but you learn fast. It must come naturally."

She reached up and pulled him back rolling on her side to bring them closer together. He could feel the warm round rise of her stomach, the pulsations of her breathing and the restless involuntary motion of her muscles. A knot rose in his throat, also a pain and he brushed his face against hers in an excess of tender demand.

"My God, how I love you." She kissed him again and this time he held her so tightly that a little moan escaped her. They parted and sat up, this time because they had to breathe.

With sudden resolution he stood up. "I really must go now, Calla. As much as I hate to, I must. I'm afraid it's dangerous for us to behave like this."

She smoothed the faded dress across her thighs and stomach, pulling it down over her knees. Her breath came in a loud shuddering sigh. "I don't know … I guess so. All I know is I'll be wanting you so it hurts till I see you again."

He pulled her to her feet and caressed her face before kissing her again. "Try to make this one last."

With a sob she went back into his arms and the pressure of her strong arms across his back was enough to make him gasp. When they broke apart her eyes were starry. "It'll have to last I guess but I wish it didn't. Why can't I go with you, Mr. Miller?"

He squeezed her shoulders. "You poor kid. Don't think I don't know what it's like. You see I love you so much that it frightens me so I know, too."

"Love …" She toyed with the word tenderly. "I never thought I'd ever hear a white man say that to me." Her heart rushed to her eyes. "And I love you, too. That must be what it is … why I cried, why I didn't want you to ever let me go … why I want to go with you."

"You can't, darling. Some day when I figure this bizarre situation all out but not now. Think you can wait?"

"I'm not sure. I'll try but I really don't know. Right now I'm despising the idea of going back to the house without you."

"Yes, I know just how you feel but it won't be too long. I promise."

That same afternoon Donna was sitting on the verandah gazing abstractly across the sun-drenched landscape when Colin dropped into a chair beside her. He had been to Silver River to confer with Bob Keller, the timber estimator. "Haven't seen you a lot lately, Donna?"

"That's right," she said shortly, "you haven't."

"Been riding today?"

She faced him, her amethyst eyes smouldering. "If you have something on your chest why beat around the bush?"

Colin was silent for a moment wondering what had her in such a frame of mind. "I didn't have anything on my mind," he said mildly. "I was just making talk."

She compressed her lips and returned to her contemplation of the landscape.

"Did you know that Ben Miller has threatened to use the picture if Charley doesn't sign the new contract?"

Her brows furrowed as she faced him. "Picture?"

"Yes, the one they snapped of you and Jack through the window that night."

She shrank back into her chair crushed and stricken. Her face was pale making her big eyes seem larger and sightless. Her breath came in fluttering gasps as she said, "How ... did you ... you ... know?"

"That doesn't matter now. Naturally, we're going to try to prevent it from getting out but I wanted you to know in case of any slip up."

She looked away, massaging her temples with her fingers. "Didn't I tell you ... didn't I say you were all wrong, that bucking that crowd would only make unhappiness?" She faced him, her face miserable and tear streaked. "Can you imagine what my life will be if that picture is ever circulated around ... *can you?*"

Colin felt misery creeping up to lump in his throat. "Of course I can," he said roughly, trying to hide the huskiness in his voice. "I wish I hadn't told you. Since I have though I'll tell you more. They'll never use it."

"How can you say that ... how can you know that?"

"Because if it comes to that I can kill Ben Miller, that's how I know it."

Her face was tortured by the lash of her emotions and her hands clenched till the fingers grew white. "You'd ... do that ... for me?"

"I'd do that for you." He reached over and touched her hand as it clenched the arm of her chair. "Don't worry about it and if it seems queer that I should warn you about it then say it'll never happen—just put it down as a suddenly born resolution. It was something I needed. I've been sitting about waiting too long as it is. What we need is some action." They were brave words but he still felt at a loss not knowing where to begin his predicted action. She rose from her chair, planted a quick kiss on his lips and disappeared into the house just as Charley swung out on his bar and dropped into his chair. "Talkin' big, ain't you?"

"Yes I am. Now that I've talked big I'll have to do something. I needed some such stimulus."

"Whut you gonna do?"

"I have an idea."

"Y'ain't a lot better off then … say ain't that the little nigger what said he wanted to work for me comin' yonder?"

Colin looked and agreed that it certainly looked like Shorty Boles but he wondered where he had gotten the jeep.

Shorty pulled up in front of the house and almost fell from the jeep in his haste. He ran swiftly up the walk and doffed his hat. "Y'all said when I fount out sumpn y'all wanted to know it. Well, I heerd Mistuh Miller tell Mistuh Beldin' dis mawnin' he was gonna hafta put de heat on you 'bout dat pulp wood. Den he sed sumpn 'bout a pitcher he was gon git made in New Orleans. He got it at de camp and he goin't' git it tonight."

Colin came to his feet with a bound. "What time tonight?"

"He didn' say. I heerd a little, den I had t' leave to go to de woods. Mistuh Prince gon' change places in de woods and he tole me t' clean up de tools whiles de others was movin'. I run off and borried Mistuh Jesse's jeep offen Mistuh Standish and come to tell y'all."

"Damn good job, Shorty," said Charley. "Here's you another twenty. If you ever get without a job come and see me." Shorty bobbed his head gratefully and grinned.

"O.K., Shorty. You'd better get back before they miss you."

Shorty departed with Willie in Colin's jeep close on his heels.

"I'll send Willie to pick up Sturges," said Colin as he came back to the verandah. "We'll take a look at that camp tonight."

"Gonna ketch Miller there?"

"That's the idea. If we can catch him there with the safe open we won't need to worry any more."

Colin got up and nervously paced the verandah. "I wonder what about the men he keeps at the camp? They could be something of an obstacle."

Charley sighed. "Wisht I had some legs. I'd sure like to git in on this deal. This part of it 'specially."

"I want in on it, too," said Donna as she came through the door. "I'm more concerned than anyone else."

They both looked at her, Charley with something like fearful regret, Colin with interest.

"This is a man's job, Donna," said the latter.

"Don't hand me that line. I've done many a man's job better than the men concerned. You'll need help and I'm going to be that help."

He shrugged. "Very well, but it might be unpleasant."

Her lip curled. "I'm accustomed to unpleasantness by now."

That afternoon Sturges went to town after conferring with Charley and Colin. There his discreet inquiries found that Miller and Belding had been together all afternoon drinking, seeming in high spirits.

He rode back to the edge of town where Colin and Donna waited for him in the jeep.

"Coast is clear, kiddies," he called as he parked near them. "I'd say let's take the long way around and approach the camp from the east side of the river. We can recon before they arrive."

The long way proved to be long and they were on the road for a good hour and a half. They stood on the bank of Silver River screened from the elaborate stone and log building on the other side by a thick growth of elder bushes.

"Well, there you are," said Sturges pointing. "I don't see any signs of life."

Colin maneuvered up and down stream for a hundred yards but still did not see anyone. "I'll have to get across," he told them, "but I don't want you two until I signal."

He drew a Colt woodsman target pistol from his waistband. "Ever use one of these, Sturges?"

"Yes. I have one and have been called pretty good with it."

"That's good. Stick it in your belt and watch sharp for me. I tried to find a log but couldn't so I'll have to swim. I'll carry my lighter in my mouth to keep it dry so I can signal with it if I have to. Donna, if there's any trouble, do you think you could get back to the jeep alone?"

"I could but I'm not."

Colin smiled. "I didn't mean that the way it sounded. If things happen it might be easier for Sturges and I to take out through the woods and not come back to the jeep. You take the key and if we get separated you go back there and wait for us. If we don't come by midnight or if you hear people, get going. We'll be all right."

"I'll deal with that when the time comes," she said through tight lips. He turned away and started down the trail and was soon hidden from their view. Just as he was about to climb down the river bank he heard a hiss. Turning he saw Donna coming toward him in a swift dogtrot. She ran up to him and hurled herself into his arms. Sobs shook her as she strove to quell them.

"What's the matter, Honey," he said stroking her soft hair tenderly.

"I've been ... mean to you ... all day. I'm afraid, Colin, dreadfully afraid."

"Then go back to the jeep and wait for us."

"I don't mean that way," she retorted fiercely. "I'm afraid you'll get hurt. You will be careful, won't you?"

He smiled and patted her shoulder. "Of course I will. You shouldn't be so concerned about me."

She clung to him with strong tenacious arms. "Can't you see I love you ... you great big hard headed dope ... can't you see that you're killing me ... turning me to water ... making a weakling of me? God, how did it ever happen?"

He drew her closer and kissed her wet hot lips with such hunger that she grew weak from the impact. "Just who told you you loved me more than I do you," he whispered fiercely, grasping a handful of thick hair and pulling her head back where he could look full into her eyes. Her lids closed forcing hot tears to flow down her face.

"Don't cry, Honey. This is the last leg we're on now—everything'll be all right. Run on back to Sturges. It's getting dark."

She crushed herself against him with painful ferocity for a second then released him. "All right," she whispered. "Please be careful."

The cold water sliding up to his armpits made Colin gasp but he continued and with his head barely above the surface swam quietly across the river until he stood erect on a narrow strip of sand. He was hidden from the house by the high bluff on which the house stood so he felt safe for the moment. For ten minutes he searched for a way to climb the forty foot bluff without using the stairway which would bring him face to face with anyone who might be about the house. Finally he located a little trail cut by cattle on their way to drink and he climbed it on all fours as silently as a cat. From the protecting screen of honeysuckle vines which wreathed the camp fence he examined the area carefully. Not a soul could he see but the smell of wood smoke came to his nostrils and toward the rear of the house he fancied he could see a blue pall indicating that someone was cooking.

Inside the fence were shrubs of various kinds affording cover of a sort but Colin was afraid to thus expose himself so soon. His caution was well taken. Through the wide front hallway of the house there stalked a huge police dog. Lazily he walked down the steps and stood looking toward the river. Then he turned and plodded back toward the kitchen. Colin tested the breeze and saw why the dog hadn't been alarmed. The wind was wrong for him to catch his scent.

Colin heard the swelling roar of a muted motor in the distance. It grew stronger and soon a big coupe slid up to the house not twenty feet from where he was hiding.

Belding and Miller got out and it was plain that they were very drunk. Miller, however, was a man of vast capacity and his driving hadn't yet been affected. He climbed out assisting Belding who had not Miller's capacity nor his sense of equilibrium.

"Whoops," yelled Miller as he reached the gate. "Beginnin' udde end, Beldin'. Beginnin' udde end."

Belding nodded owlishly. "Shure is palopal. Beginnin' …" He hiccoughed so violently that only Miller's strong arm prevented him from falling.

"Lookout 'ere, Beld'n, sonvbitch you. Faw down inna minnit."

Belding giggled. "Whroo … wrup, whoo gives a dam. Temme that, whr … who gives a dam."

"Eddie," bellowed Miller lurching toward the kitchen. "Blag bastud … Y'got some supper ready?"

Eddie put his head out of the window. "Yassuh, sho is." "You tell them other boys t' take th' night off?"

"Yassuh. Dey all gone t' town."

"Y' good nigger, Eddie. Me 'n Mistuh Beld'n 'll be in the livn rum. Bring in a bottle and some cokes 'n ice 'n stuff."

"Yassuh."

Colin grinned. This was almost too good. Miller and Belding drunk and no one else here but a colored cook. Still grinning he made his way back to the little beach and from the protection of the bluff struck a light and waved it in wide arcs. Across the river came a very creditable imitation of an owl. Colin withdrew to the deeper shadows of a clump of overhanging Virginia creeper and with a prayer that there was no poison ivy in it sat down and waited.

It took Sturges and Donna some fifteen minutes to make the crossing due to their redoubled caution initiated by the sight of lights coming on in the house.

"What's the dope?" asked Sturges as he stepped up on the little beach, dripping, followed by Donna.

"Your Dad and Belding ... both pretty drunk. Only the Negro cook, Eddie, here. The others are all in town. The set-up looks so good that I'm beginning to suspect it's too easy."

Sturges grunted. "Never look a gift horse in the mouth."

"It won't be a gift horse any way you look at it. There's a regular lion of a dog there. He's the next problem."

Sturges whistled soundlessly. "I'd forgotten about him. He's bad medicine. That's why Dad keeps him here."

"What is the next step?" asked Donna, shifting nervously on her feet.

"The next step is to get that dog. Just how we'll do that is something which I'm ready to accept suggestions on."

"I can put on the damndest cat fight you ever heard," said Donna hopefully.

Sturges perked up. "That sounds good to me. It might make him investigate."

He nodded. "Donna's going to pull her part yet." He squeezed her shoulders. "Come over here where the fence approaches the bluff. We want to get the dog outside so we can dispose of him. Do you suppose we could risk a twenty-two shot?"

"With them drunk," put in Donna, "Eddie is the only one likely to hear it. I think it's worth the risk. It's a cinch we can't do anything till the dog is taken care of."

Wolf lay on the ground near the kitchen door and gnawed on a succulent bone which he had wheedled from Eddie. He heard the cat the first time and raised his head, his ears pricking up. A second cry came to his ears and he heaved spasmodically with a bark that didn't quite come out. The meows were repeated separately a few more times then the cats got together in a spitting screeching melee that made the air ring. Leaping to his feet he let go a thunderous bark and he leaped in the direction of the sounds. When he neared the fence the sound suddenly stopped and so did the dog. He sniffed the air and the scent he caught was not that of cats. The bristles rose on his neck and he took two more steps then froze to let his nose tell the story.

Colin, his hand resting on the top of a weathered locust post, took careful aim with the Woodsman. There was a sharp crack and Wolf crumpled to the ground without a sound. Tossing the gun to Donna Colin leaped the fence with one mighty spring, his hand using the post as a lever. Stooping he caught the dog by the hind legs and with a heave sent him soaring out over the bluff to drop with a muffled splash into the river. Then he went over the fence again and together they sat behind the honeysuckle vines.

Eddie came to the front porch and looked fearfully around, then went into the living room where the two men drank and guffawed at nothing.

"Mist Miller ... y'all hear a shot o' sum kind?"

"Shot ... shot?" Miller looked at him with heavy gravity. "What you been drinkin', Eddie. Been in my licker again'? Tole you I'd skin you 'live if I ever caught you … Shot he says, Beld'n. Shot … well, you're half shot, Beld'n. So's Eddie. Goddamit, Eddie, go git us some supper … starvin'."

Eddie wandered back to the kitchen and went into the back yard calling for Wolf in a hushed urgent voice. "Hyer Wolf … come hyer boy. I gotta nother bone fer you."

A noise in the bushes near the fence sent him scuttling back to the kitchen where he banged the door and stood trembling and sweating. The boss could act casual about that shot but Eddie had heard it and Eddie had been shot *at* too many times to be mistaken. One thing certain, he was not going stumbling around in the dark looking for any signs of the shooter. With this to comfort him he barred the kitchen door and in spite of the heat from the stove he pulled the shutter of the window to and barred it also. Thus fortified he turned to the supper again which was about ready to be served.

Belding and Miller ate greedily like underfed swine dropping gravy and driblets of other foods on their shirt fronts, mopping at them halfheartedly with snowy napkins which soon became spotted and filthy.

Eddie whose courage hadn't risen much decided to try again. "I hyeered dat shot jes' like I'm tellin' you. Dey was a cat fight out in de front and Wolf went to see 'bout hit. De shot come den and I ain't seen him since."

They growled at him, reiterated their belief that he had been hitting the bottle and anyhow there were no cats around here, which fact sank home in Eddie's fluttering breast like a dull arrow from a powerful bow. If there were no cats about then it hadn't been cats that he had heard … Sounded like cats. He went back into the kitchen and assuaged his nerves with a bottle of gin. So assiduously did he treat them that he began to notice that the kitchen was tilted to a highly improbable angle and while pondering over this problem of outraged physics, since there were no dishes falling, he went to sleep.

After the off note rendition of several songs, off color, and the recital of the *French Stenographer,* even more off color, Miller grew tired.

"Le's gedda pitcher and g'home," he muttered.

"Okay," agreed Belding, trying to get up from the table and falling flat.

"Y' pushed me," he complained, getting up with a noticeable list.

"I did'n do it," denied Miller, wheezing with mirth.

Together they went into another room which had a large fireplace that seemed odd in that it did not correspond with any chimney in the house.

Through the window Colin watched, Sturges and Donna crowding up close behind him. They had crept all around the house and seeing that Eddie was fast asleep grew incautious.

Miller twisted an ornament on the mantel and the fireplace began slowly to revolve. Colin could see that the safe was behind the false fireplace and the whole thing revolved on a turntable. Neat and handy. As Miller worked out the combination, Colin slipped on a black ski cap over his head pulling it down until it covered his face. Holes had been cut for the eyes, the whole thing giving him a sinister Mephistophelian look. Miller extracted a big manila envelope from a drawer in the safe and together they sat about the table.

"Hoddam," ejaculated Belding as he gazed at one of the biggest prints. "Boyoboy ... whadda woman."

Colin felt Donna's fingers dig hard into the muscles of his left arm. He reached around and patted her hand gently, then backing up about ten paces took a running start and with a prodigious bound cleared the shrubs and leapfrogged through the big open window into the room striking the floor on both feet. With a smooth fluid motion a forty-five appeared in his hand and clattered with metallic wickedness as he worked a cartridge into the chamber.

"You will put your hands over your head."

Both Miller and Belding did a fast bit of sobering that must have been painful. Miller's face looked like unbaked bread while Belding looked sobered and punchy at the same time.

Colin scooped up the negative and prints and striking a light built a fire of them on the shiny surface of the cedar table. When the last vestige of fire had disappeared he looked at them. "I want the rest of the prints," he said.

"There ain't any more," said Miller.

Colin hit him a hard blow on the mouth with his left fist. Miller went over backward with a crash and was kicked to his feet by the toe of Colin's right foot.

"The other prints," he ground out again.

" 'Fore God there ain't no more prints," screamed Belding, spittle spilling from his slack mouth. Again the hard fist cracked and this time Belding crashed to the floor and was kicked erect again.

"I'm tired playing around," Colin ground out. "I'll give you, Miller, two seconds to cough up the other prints." He cocked the hammer of his pistol back slowly and lined it up with the lobe of Miller's left ear. "One."

"Jesus Christ," screamed Miller livid with terror. "I tell you there ain't no more prints." Inside the room the pistol thundered like a field gun. Miller slumped forward in his chair his head hitting the table resoundingly. A raspy keening noise came from Belding's strutted throat as he switched his stricken gaze from the fallen Miller to the steady leering barrel of the gun which drooled a tendril of gossamer smoke. His hands fluttered spasmodically like the wings of a dying quail beating a tattoo on the table top. Saliva dropped in stringing ropes from his mouth. His eyes popped and suddenly his nerves revolted and he went slack sliding from the chair to strike the floor with a thud.

Colin grinned and lifted Miller's head by its hair. A tiny blob of blood showed where the bullet had nicked the lobe of his ear.

Miller gasped and shaking his head slowly pushed himself back to a sitting position. His breath came in rattling bubbles and he coughed to clear his throat of a collection of phlegm. Tears streaked his face and he blubbered like a whipped child.

"Please, sir, we're tellin' you the truth. This is all the prints ... so help me God." Miller crossed himself to make the statement take on weight but performed the gesture incorrectly.

Colin grinned. "O.K., if you say so but I'm telling you if I ever hear ..." He stopped and froze. A door had opened from the living room, and Sheriff Potter stood in the door, a gun in his hand.

"You'll do what, Mr. Campbell? Never mind that now. Let's see you drop your gun for now, then we'll talk."

Colin opened his hand and the gun slipped to the floor. The sob of relief and returning rage swelled from Miller like the murmur of a crowd.

"Kill the son of a bitch, Potter. What're you standing there like that for ..."

"Reasons, Ben. This is fun. I didn't come here for this but just look." He walked over and nudged Belding with his foot. "The greats have fallen." He looked at the ashes on the table. "Well, our last weapon gone up in flames. Too bad. I'm afraid I must also go up but I'll go up in a plane and when I do I will not be alone." He walked to the safe and opened a large drawer. "I'll just take yours, Miller. Belding will split with you I'm sure."

With a roar Miller came to his feet and lunged at Potter who calmly shot him three times in the chest and stomach. "Please, no moves, Mr. Campbell. I shall need you further because I want your plane."

Potter withdrew the drawer and put it on the table. This also placed his back toward the living room door. He picked up several packets of bills. "Hundreds and thousands," he said gloatingly. "In Europe I shall be a Kahn."

Colin wondered at the loss of Potter's hayseed speech.

"I also know a certain non-skid route where too many questions are not asked which lands at Dakar. Nice place, Dakar … to land anyhow. I won't be there long. I …"

Potter went to the floor with a crash that shook the stout house. Donna stood over him with the .22 pistol in her hand.

Colin sighed and retrieved his automatic. "I was afraid to look because I thought he might see something in my eyes."

Sturges came through the window holding Donna's .32 revolver. "She didn't want to hurt her gun, Colin, so she used yours. Is … is the old man dead?"

"Yes," Colin bent over and tried to find a pulse but could not. "Yes," he said again. "Sorry, fella."

Sturges sighed and shrugged. "I should be, I guess …" He didn't finish. He lifted the cringing Belding into a chair. "Belding, you have a chance to do something right for once in your life." Sturges' voice was hard and authoritative.

"Did you see Potter shoot Dad?"

Belding nodded. "I had just come to."

"That's good. The story will be this. We've never been here. Potter came while you and Dad were opening the safe and he tried to hold you up. You pretended to faint but Dad got truculent and Potter shot him. While he was at the safe you conked him on the head. You'll have saved your money. You'll be something of a hero and you'll escape a charge of blackmail and of course if the Treasury Department knew of this safe you …"

"I'll do it, I'll do it," boomed Belding almost beside himself with joy at the prospect of getting through scot free. "You people won't peach on me … I mean if I do like you say?"

"On what's here now we won't, Belding," said Colin coming into the conversation. "But I'd advise you to pay your income tax from now on."

"Thank you, Mr. Campbell … I guess you're being pretty swell being from Washington and all …"

Colin smiled and jerked the cap from his face. "Yes, I think I'm being pretty swell all right but I can change any time I need to."

They bound Potter hand and foot and put him in the trunk of Miller's coupe. Belding was to take him in, make out a charge and send the coroner in for Miller's body. When he left he was grinning broadly.

"There's a man who recovers in a hurry," said Donna. She began to tremble like a leaf and had to sit on the ground. "I'm bushed," she said weakly. "I guess you were right, Colin. Swimming rivers, creeping about in the dark, shooting dogs and conking people is a man's game."

Colin lifted her easily and carried her into the living room. He poured her a stiff drink as well as one for himself and Sturges. They drank, avoiding any reference to what lay in the other room. "Why did you let Donna come in and sap Potter," asked Colin accusingly.

Sturges shrugged. "She said something might happen and if it did then she wanted someone outside who could shoot. She claims she can't and her reasoning made sense. Her sapping ability stands well established. A little harder and there'd be no trial for Denny."

They had several drinks and Donna began to feel exultant. "Let's go and take the bottle with us."

"I might have thought of that idea," said Colin.

Two hours and any number of drinks later they were sitting in the jeep beneath the big oak in front of the house.

"If we weren't wet we could just stay here," said Donna stretching luxuriously. "If I felt any better I'd have to be three people."

"We might catch our death."

"Will you carry me?"

"Sure."

"All the way across the doorway?"

"Right."

"Know what it'll mean."

"Right."

"When?"

"Any day you say."

When he picked her up she clung to him and her warmth started his blood racing. Later when they had showered and he found that he was not alone in his room it redoubled its speed.

She was a shaft of tan fire and the touch of her skin sent his nerves into rapturous knots. To him she seemed to emanate a kind of radiation, not necessarily of heat but something that reached deeply within him and set up an urge that rolled steadily down on him gathering speed and energy. Her hands dug into the loose skin beneath his arms and gripped him painfully. With a surge of power he lifted her to the bed and buried his face in the exciting valley between her breasts, letting the tiger in him loose, reveling in the insurgent reaction it set in motion.

Sturges arrived at the tower shack and when he opened the door he found that he too had company. He shook her gently by the shoulder. "Wake up princess."

Her eyes opened languidly and as they took him in a smile roughed her lips making her face light up in a manner that never failed to fascinate him.

"Why did you come?" His voice was hoarse and forced.

She palmed a delicate yawn and sat up, smiling in his face with such brilliance that he felt a little unnerved. "Because I wanted to."

This was the sort of answer he might have expected but he hadn't expected it to be delivered with such brutal bluntness and he was figuratively rocked upon his heels.

He said, "But people might not …"

"No one knows about it, Mr. Miller. That is, except you and me and Mother and maybe Marny and Rose."

He was thereby placed in the position of being obviously the only person who could object. The night was cool but he could feel beads of sweat coming to his brow. His pulse began to thunder in his ears and her closeness was more intoxicating than the whiskey he had drunk.

She stood up and coming close to him placed her hand on his head and gently massaged his hair. His arms went around her waist and he buried his face in her soft stomach. She clutched his head and held him close for a moment then bent over and kissed the nape of his neck. Had she touched him with a hot wire the effect wouldn't have been more electric. He felt scorched, then very weak. She slid into his lap and holding his face in her two hands kissed him with such unutterable tenderness that tears stung his eyes and he bowed his head to hide them.

"You do love me, don't you, Calla?" It was as much a plea as a question.

She smiled and shook her head chidingly. "Don't you know by now?"

He nodded, feeling very humble and at the same time very proud. "Yes, I guess I do. I'd be a fool if I didn't."

Again she kissed him and this time with such heady passion that his returning clutch was sheer reflex. He swung her over into the crook of his left arm, cradling her, the roving touch of her lips sending flames of desire over his body. He cupped her left breast with his hand and as he did so she suddenly broke away, her head arching back, her hand covering his pressing it down hard. Her breath came in gasps and her body trembled and writhed ever so slightly.

With feverish insistence his hand tore at the buttons on her dress front, flinging back the obscuring cloth to reveal the trembling mound of flesh of such maddening beauty that for a moment he could only stare. He bent over and kissed the throbbing tip, his head whirling with an onslaught of emotion. She arched herself across his lap with a strangled moan as if in pain, her hands clutching aimlessly at his clothes, her long hair sweeping the floor. With a sudden motion he lifted her, dropped her roughly on the bed, falling to his knees beside her, buried his head beside hers shivering and weak. "No, Calla … no, no, no!"

She clutched him by the shoulders and lifted him by main strength. Her hair was wild and half obscuring her vision, making her look like a lovely pagan. Her eyes flashed and she strained him to her breast with frenzied strength. "Yes, yes, yes … if you love me, *yes!*"

His face grew calmer and his brain clearer. What was he about to toss carelessly away under the pretense of … what? He was suddenly chilled with the conviction that if he stopped now she'd hate him with the same unalloyed violence that she loved him. He pulled her to her feet and kissed her, at the same time slipping her simple dress from her shoulders. It caught at her waist and again he urged it further till finally she stood crushed to him naked, warm and pulsating with life, love and such devastating passion that he suffered a twinge of fear. He laid her gently on the bunk.

When he awoke sunlight was pouring through the window over their heads, casting a spray of golden dust on the rough wooden floor. The sight of Calla sleeping uncovered beside him again brought moisture to his eyes and a lump to his throat. He could *not* make a casual mistress of the girl. He had swept her off her feet and her simple nature had responded in the only way it could. She had sought him through an urge that was greater than she and he had let things progress until there was no turning back, at least until there was greater danger in so doing than continuing. His sigh was so deep that she woke, her eyes sweeping her unfamiliar surroundings at first with question, then comprehension. He noticed that they showed no fear.

She pulled him to her so that their bodies pressed closely together. Her mouth wandered over his face like a live thing softly playing with his lips and eyes and all the while she crooned little birdlike notes which were not words but more expressive than mere words could ever be. He stroked the satin perfection of her back and thigh until she closed her eyes and a hard rigor possessed her. She pressed herself against him, her body moving with an urge no mortal man could deny.

Sturges balanced a coffee cup without a handle in his big hand and eyed her across the rough table. The breakfast had been bountiful and delicious.

"Sweet, what'll become of us?" He was deadly serious.

Her eyes darkened. "Mother says we are all like her. We never think of tomorrow. We only live for today. Maybe I'm a little different. I do think of tomorrow except that I can't see any tomorrow for you and I and my mind sort of shuts up on me because without you I don't even want to see tomorrow. I couldn't stand it, Mr. Miller … I really couldn't. I know I must sound dramatic or maybe young and silly but I mean that."

"I have no doubt that you mean it," he assured her. "As for me …" He stopped and considered, tried to picture himself without her, out of his life … gone beyond recall. He began to sweat again. He couldn't do it. His eyes raised to hers. "There'll be no tomorrow, Calla, without us—together."

The gladness in her face struck him like a knife because he did not know how he was to accomplish his brave words. She came around the table and sat in his lap, her quick kiss salty from the tears of her gratitude.

The strength of his clasp showed something of the storm that raged within him. Roughly he shook his head. "You'll have to go now. I'll take you. No one must know you've been here."

She bounced up and smiled. "I'll go but I won't stay away."

"You won't have to," he said huskily. "You won't have to."

CHAPTER ELEVEN

BELDING, ROBERTS AND Semple sat on the broad verandah looked like small frightened children. Charley was triumphant, hard and inclined to be a little vindictive.

"So there she is. Take 'er or leave 'er. It don't make a two penny damn to me which. That there's the contract and if you'll notice, Semple, I got Colin t' tack a clause on there what says I kin terminate the deal at my very own pleasure, and brother just *any* of you bums try to shave a corner … much as a skeeter and see. 'Nother thing, I don't want John Prince walkin' 'round on my land. Git 'im offen it 'fore I loses my temper and kills the bastard. If they hadn't of sweated the name of the deppity what shot George outa Potter, I had Prince all picked for the rap."

Mr. Semple puffed out his cheeks and hacked importantly. "But look here, Charley, that's high handed and unreasonable. We can't …"

"Shut up," bellowed Belding, turning the color of a ripe watermelon. "We got you here to see to the *legal* angle of this here deal. You ain't got no paper mill and you ain't handlin' this deal at all so keep your trap shut." He turned to Charley. 'That all, Mr. Taradon?"

"That's all fer now. Might think up somethin' later."

Belding nodded and brought out a huge fountain pen. "Then it's good enough for me. You got the wood and we got the mill. I think we can get along."

" 'Course we kin," said Charley relenting somewhat "Always could of. You people didn't want to."

"The leopard's done changed his spots," said Belding with a wry smile. "I want to get along."

Roberts looking immeasurably relieved, cleared the ashes from his throat. "And I also. I haven't felt this good in years."

"What sort of deal will you make with Mrs. Miller?" asked Colin.

Belding having signed the contract passed it to Roberts. "Oh, she was plenty willin' to sell out. She had her belly full of Silver River. Shouldn't be surprised to see her at some political meetin's somewheres before long ridin' in Renshaw's automobile. She wanted to know where she could get in touch with him when we bought her out the other day."

When they had gone Charley and Colin sat in silence for a long time. Finally Charley squirmed about to face the other. "Son, I ain't very good at thankin' people ..."

"Then don't do it," interrupted Colin. "You'd embarrass us both."

Charley hoisted himself to the shelf and bit into a plug of Brown's Mule with gusto. "Much obliged. They's some things I ain't a bit of good at. What's this business about you bein' from Washington?"

Colin grinned. "Mostly stuff. I did a little work for the Forestry Division right after I got out of the Army. I was so unimportant that no one could find anything out. That's what made me so mysterious. I know a few kids up there and some janitors, a bartender or two and some fairly cute chicks. Otherwise, I'm still a lad reared in a big city who got sick of it and wanted the big outdoors."

"What'll you do now?"

"Can't say. Actually I hadn't thought about it. Too many other things on my mind. This deal we just killed, forestry and I must admit—Donna."

Charley spat into the yard and grinned. "I notice you ain't admittin' it but didn't you have Rose on your mind a leetle bit?"

Colin flushed. "Yes I did." He ran his fingers through his hair and breathed heavily. "I've got to do something about that."

"Like as to how?"

"I don't know. If I was superstitious I'd say that they're a family of witches. Rose is too young to know the things she knows."

"Son, nigger women's had white men by the———fer two hundred years. I don't know what it is but it sure is sumpn. I could read you a story 'bout near ev'ry white family in these here parts and the best 'un'd be on me. Now I'm gonna ax you a question … if I'd ax it to a lot o' men it'd git me kilt … Do you love that Rose gal?"

Colin shook his head. "No, I don't know. I have a tremendous lot of affection for her and I like her … I feel sorry for her but I don't love her. I'm afraid though that her color has little or nothing to do with it. Sturges has just proved my point there."

Charley's eyebrows arched with question. "Come again?"

"Sturges is absolutely wild about Calla. I mean positively nuts."

Charley sighed. "I knowed it was bound to happen and thank God it happened to a *man* and not some mousy son of a bitch like her daddy. Them kids didn't ask fer the life they're livin'."

Colin cracked his knuckles distractedly. "I only wish there was something I could do for them."

"Like what f'r instance?"

"Send the girls to school … nursing school or something. Any of them could pass any test that they'd take. Their mother has seen to that."

"Let's go back a ways," said Charley with a queer ring in his voice. "Want to work fer me permanent?"

Colin sat up. "Charley, I like you and I think you like me. There has to be a better reason than that for any such move."

"If they ain't and if you can't see what it is then you just want to be tole so's to git your hair slicked up."

"O.K.," said Colin with a smile. "So I want my ego pumped. Go ahead and tell me."

Charley enumerated on his fingers. "Fust, yer a man—a man's man. Y' got sense and y' got a heart in you. Oh, hell, you're weak about in spots where most of us is, but that's the man in you. Secont, you got a feelin' fer woods. I know, I got it myself. I watched you the fust day I seen you look at 'em good. Third, I'm an old man. I'm strong and manage to git around but the year two thousand'll find me in just the condition I was in 'fore I was born. I'll be around some time I hope and plague the hell out of everybody but I ain't fer always—you know that. Donna's a good kid but she's flighty and needs a steady hand. Fourth, you love 'er. If I run you off I'd have to put up with you anyhow so seems to me the sensible thing is to have you under foot where I kin keep an eye on you."

Colin nodded. "That's enough. I'm sold."

That night Charley excused himself early and left Donna and Colin sitting on the verandah. Donna broke the silence first. "Were you drunk the other night, Colin, or did you mean what you said when you brought me in the house?"

She wore a simple white dress that fitted in a manner calculated to disturb the breathing of any male who chanced to see her. A faint woodsy fragrance drifted toward him that he knew to be perfume but could not identify. It seemed to be a scent that she might have emanated physically. As she spoke his mind flitted to Rose and his reply was not immediately forthcoming.

"So you didn't mean it?" She faced him, her eyes dark with anger and her body taut.

"Honey, if you just want an excuse to get mad then go ahead and throw one," he said quietly. "I was just trying to answer you in the most graceful way. As for meaning what I said ... certainly. I meant every word of it."

"Then why all the hesitation now?"

"Well, what exactly do you know of me?"

"I know everything I want to know."

She was sounding a little too much like Rose for comfort. "You know less than nothing about me. You know my name and a few inconsequential ..."

"Colin Campbell, you make me *sick*. Are you the only one in the world who has any sense? Don't you give me any credit at all? You think you know everything about me and I don't know a thing about you?"

"Touché," he said weakly. "No, I guess I didn't mean all that."

"Then what do you mean?"

"I have a weakness," he said carefully, "that I have just discovered. I'm ..."

"Now your protests are one thing," she continued with her whiplash voice, "but your feelings are another. If you want out I'm not going to hog tie you."

Colin came erect stung from his lethargic retirement. "I have neither said nor intimated that I wanted out." His voice was harsh.

"Then why all this muck about your past? What did you expect to accomplish by it?"

"Let's not say any more about it. Time you were in bed anyway."

Colin bathed leisurely that night and when he came back in the room he stopped short. She was there and as before the sight of her sent a thundering burst of blood pounding out its song of passion in his ears. "This can't go on every night," he whispered with a marked lack of conviction.

The next morning at breakfast Charley said to Colin, "Son, I been figurin'. You fix it with them kids 'bout what they want to do, school and such, and I'll foot the bill."

"That's white of you Charley but let's split it. I'm not broke."

"Nope … I got more'n you … betcha. I'm just too old and growed to my chair to know how t' spend it. You spend it for me."

He waylaid Donna in the hall after breakfast and kissed her with such finesse and passion that she clung to him weakly and shook her head angrily. "Dammit, you always make me go weak and shuddery inside when you do that. Speaking of such, who is Sturges in love with?"

He held her away from him. "Who told you that?"

"I know Sturges. Any man who wouldn't even turn his head to look at me soaking wet climbing out of the creek has lost his mind for some woman and I do mean lost."

"Your sudden display of penetration staggers me. Sturges met Rose's sister in the woods the other day and he went under like a lead marble."

She ran her arm through his. "Let's go out on the verandah. I've seen Calla and I know what you mean. I think I'm pretty good to look at but that girl is someone I wouldn't want to go up against."

Colin sat and looked at her for a long moment. "You know, I find it just a little hard to credit my senses thinking about you and Charley. There aren't supposed to be people like you in the South."

"That's what a lot of yankees would find out if they took the trouble. You mean my attitude about Sturges and Calla?"

"Yes … that and a few other things."

She shrugged. "He's bitten off a healthy chew and I don't know how he figures to swing it but he'll do it some way. Sturges sort of went to seed when he came back from college till you bucked him up but he has a terrible lot of intense stuff in him. If he really loves Calla, and if I know him he does, then we can say goodbye to Sturges and Calla."

"Why do you say that?"

"Because he'll have none of this house-in-the-woods stuff. He has a hard streak of what we have become accustomed to call honor as odd as it might sound what with this and that but he has it. He'll never make a mistress of her. Of course, it will change the order of his life."

"That won't worry him too much," said Colin. "The present order was what drove him to drink."

Sturges Miller strode toward the Stuerm cabin like a man with a mission. Calla saw him coming and ran to meet him throwing herself into his arms with a little sob of gladness and for a long moment he held her hungrily oblivious of the tittering of numerous children and the rapt stares of Marny and Rose. They parted and walked toward the house arm in arm.

Irma met him at the steps and shook his hands. Her eyes were suspiciously wet but her voice was steady. "Ordinarily, Mr. Miller, I'm opposed to demonstrations but I wouldn't take a year of my life for what I just saw."

"Thank you, Irma. I've come to talk with you about Calla."

Irma made a barely perceptible motion of her hand and children melted away like magic. "No, Calla," she said. "This concerns you so you stay."

Sturges took a chair and sat heavily. "You knew Calla was coming to my cabin the other night, Irma?"

"Yes, sir."

"Then you approve of her doing that?"

"Let us say I approved of her reasons for doing it, Mr. Miller. If you mean that I deliberately suggested that she do so in order to place some responsibility on you, I did not and her reasons were not those of a scheming woman."

"What were her reasons?"

Irma sighed and clenched her toil-hardened hands in her lap. "The only excuse for the closest communion between man and woman is love. I don't say that in a narrow sense. If a man sleeps with a woman—pardon the blunt term—and comes back again and again he, in any good definition of the word, is in love with her. In some cases we can even say that he is in love with her only during their association and forgets it when he leaves. I say that to take care of some of the exceptions you are thinking about. Actually he doesn't forget or he wouldn't return. If a man sleeps with a woman whom he does not love he has accomplished a conquest which was all he wanted in the first place. He'll never come back unless the fates cast her in his path. He is either an opportunist or an adventurer but even he is not immune because even adventurers tire of their adventures and turn to the one woman. Calla is a woman. A woman in a very tightly knit set of adverse circumstances. In all truth, Mr. Miller, how else was she to know if you really loved her? How was she to know that what you felt was not something built up in your mind that might crumple with the first breeze that blew? I've seen her since and I've seen you. I've seen you together. I know and I'm satisfied."

Sturges kneaded his hands distractedly. "But how did you know it would turn out this way? How did you know that I wouldn't think she was just a loose woman on the make?"

"Because I think you are an intelligent man, Mr. Miller, and because *Calla doesn't know the first thing about how a loose woman on the make would act.*"

He was silent for a long time. "I'll learn some day," he said huskily, "never to lock horns with you on anything, Irma. I don't mean this to sound flip or disrespectful but in my cabin the other night Calla was not of this world. I would choke on my own spit if I attempted to tell you what sublime beauty, the unutterable tenderness … oh, hell, I just can't tell you."

Calla, who had been a silent listener, bent her head slowly.

"You don't have to tell me, Mr. Miller. You see, I saw her after you brought her back. Such things are not obvious to men but they are to women. No woman can lie with her lover beautifully, poetically, with full completion and musical concord and not show it. She was a pearl, sir, a gem. She was never more beautiful than that moment when she walked in the house."

He nodded his head in agreement. "Yes," he said softly, "I know."

He sat up straight. "What I came to say, Irma, is this. There'll be no woodland assignations for us, no hidden cabin, no nocturnal scuttlings. We're going away. When I graduated I had an offer from the University of California to teach psychology. It might still be open. I'll have some money from my father's estate and whether I get the job or not we'll leave. We'll marry like people are supposed to do and we'll rear a family. We want Rose or Marny to come to us as soon as we get a place to stay. That'll take the immediate pressure off you and then later on maybe we can take more of them. I'm saying this because I don't think you want to leave."

"You are right, sir. I won't leave and I want all my children to reach maturity here. You don't know how I honor you for your understanding of us, your consideration and what you are doing for Calla. I probably don't deserve this."

Calla spoke. "When are we leaving, Mr. Miller?"

Sturges turned and faced her. "Don't ever call me that again," he said in an odd voice. "I can't imagine what I was thinking about allowing it to go on this long."

Irma chuckled. "Habit is a strong thing. You allowed it because you had received it all your life. She did it because she has learned to."

"Anyway, Calla," he continued, "we'll go as soon as I can get the estate cleared up. I'll move back to the house tomorrow and get Semple to probate the will as soon as possible. I understand that my stepmother is so anxious to leave Silver Creek that she'll agree to anything reasonable."

"You'll come back often," her voice was small and entreating.

He stood and touched her cheek gently. "Every day, my dear—every day. There's a lot of things we will have to work out, clothes being high on the list."

Colin drove his jeep to the hillside and stopped beneath the gum tree. He had only a short time to wait. Rose trotted from the brush in a pair of crimson shorts and a short sleeveless jacket that seemed about to burst its buttons. She walked to the jeep, placed her hands on the vehicle and smiled at him. "Good morning, Mr. Campbell."

"Good morning, Rose, I suppose you heard the jeep again?"

"Yes, sir."

"Come sit down. I want to talk to you." She obediently came around and climbed in.

"What do you want to be when you grow up, Rose?"

She pondered a moment. "I've always wanted to be a lady."

A slow pain came into his throat and he looked out across the woods shimmering in the heat. "Didn't you ever want to be a teacher or a nurse or ..."

"Marny is just dying to be a nurse."

"And you just want to be a lady?"

"Yes, sir."

He was stumped at this end anyhow so he sought another subject. "This is the last time I'll see you, Rose. I'm going to marry Miss Donna."

"Oh, I'm glad, Mr. Campbell. She's so nice."

He beat the steering wheel softly wishing that a storm would come or an earthquake or something equally violent. His conversations with Rose always left him veering in a most upsetting way. "You see," he continued desperately, "I couldn't come any more after I'm married."

"No, sir."

He nearly lost his temper. "What the hell do you mean, 'no, sir'?"

He didn't frighten her in the least, instead she stretched her arms overhead, drawing her silken legs beneath her and thrusting her breasts against their frail covering, making his head ring with a queer pumping tempo.

"I mean you'll stop seeing me, Mr. Campbell—that's what you said, wasn't it?"

"Yes, that's what I said and don't you try hexing me. again. It won't work."

She faced him half in jest and half seriously. "Do you really believe that?"

He dashed a lock of pale hair from his forehead and cursed hard and low. "I don't know what I believe."

She came nearer and when her breasts touched his shoulder he cursed again and took her in his arms. Five minutes later, winded and not more than a third conscious, Colin sat up. She touched his face gently with her hands. "The creek is that way, Mr. Campbell."

Again he cursed but he shifted gears and rolled down the hill.

CHAPTER TWELVE

"IF YOU COME here to spill a lot o' thanks you can turn around and go home." Charley was testy in his efforts to stem what he thought might be an embarrassing moment.

Sturges walked up the steps grinning and took a chair. "Wasn't gonna say a thing about thanks. I was going to tell you a story."

"Whut sorta story?"

"Oh, about some people I knew once. They were pretty swell people because they managed to get a fellow straight with himself and after he was chased out of his own home they gave him a place to sleep and a job to do. He is very grateful."

Charley sniffed. "Fairy tale. I can't hear you."

"I just dropped by. Colin and Donna are gone and I wanted to see them but you'll tell them won't you ..."

"Sure," said Charley softly. "Go ahead son. They'll understand ... I'll tell 'em."

The moon cast bizarre shadows over the pasture and where there were no shadows a pall of silver dust covered the grass. Charley sat on his shelf and spat carefully away from the rose bush, Donna being within easy reach. He turned around and hoisted himself back into his chair. "When you two gonna stop this night-time tippin' 'round and git married?"

They both blushed and sank back into their chairs with such a beaten look that Charley cackled with glee.

"Bet you thought you was gettin' away with sumpn didn't you? But I figgered you'd make it permanent sooner or later." He grinned and hurled his tobacco into the yard, enjoying their acute embarrassment.

"Well, take your time … No hurry." He swung aloft on his bars and disappeared into the hall.

Colin let the air go from his lungs in a bursting sigh. "I think we'd better go get a license."

Donna closed her eyes and nodded. "Me too. I mean, Amen."